Until We Sleep

James B. Christensen

Ravensbook

ALSO BY JAMES B. CHRISTENSEN:

For everyone who keeps going...

"Can two walk together, except they be agreed?"
Amos 3:3 (KJV).

COLBY

There was much to escape from that summer, the summer the world became new. The early days of the season, when spring had released its chilly grip on mornings and evenings, were ordinary days, and escape from life's pressures was still possible. A vacation to a beautiful, quiet place by the sea could provide refuge for a week or two. Real life was forgotten in walks through gentle, lapping waves and leisurely dinners in the long shadows and honey-filtered glow of an evening sun. After introspective rest, you could return to home and work and face the fret and froth of a troubled world with renewed strength. But before this vacation could end, there was no escape from anything, anywhere. I didn't appreciate the dull routine of family until it was gone.

These memories begin in the backseat of the family's Lincoln Navigator on the trip from Seattle to the Swanson family vacation home on the Washington coast. The Blue Lady is what she was called, not just because of the cloak of sky blue paint she wore, but also after a ghostly lady dressed in blue that was first seen wandering the house and grounds in the time of my great-grandfather, Eldon Swanson. I called her "The Swanson" because I was nineteen and immature. My dad said I was welcome to call her that as long as I didn't mind sleeping in her dank, dungeon-like basement. So, after that, I called her by her proper name.

My sisters, Madison, 12, and Sophia, 14, had the middle row. When they weren't on their phones, they chattered like overly-caffeinated blue jays, asking Mom and Dad endless questions about out-of-the-blue topics. I remember they asked how boats could float, if God ever got an itch, and Dad's favorite Billie Eilish song. "Never heard of him," was Dad's answer.

My dad, Leo, and mom, Robyn, were in their mid-forties. Dad gave few hints he had any dissatisfaction with his life. He was ex-Army. With the engineering skills they gave him and an MIT degree via the GI Bill, he quickly built a large firm designing bridges, roads, and other things beyond my comprehension. He made big money doing what he loved. He gave me that lesson by word and example--find something you love and get cracking.

Mom had been more or less comfortable with her state of being, but she was ready for radical change and had talked to me about it before we left. She wanted out of the city. After the pandemic craziness and riots converged at once, put together with crime that festered and spread with impunity, she felt a constant spiritual sickness that she worried would take her completely, not to mention the fear she carried about her children's futures. She worked at a library because it was quiet.

Seeing the back of Mom and Dad's heads as they rode in front was an enduring memory. Dad had short gray hair. He was athletic for his age, still able to kick some ass if needed. Mom's blonde hair had been short for as long as I could remember. She found a way to keep her style different and exciting. She was sweet and tough, and Dad always talked about how her green eyes left him helpless. The older I got, the more I saw what a good thing they had and wished for it myself someday.

As I mentioned, Mom wanted the family to leave the city. We had a lot of money. Dad could sell his firm for a mint. We could live any way we wanted. Together, my folks had built up enough success to choose any new start, and Mom was ready to do so. Her goal on this trip was to lean on Dad to retire and permanently move the clan to the Blue Lady.

That was going to take some convincing. Dad didn't sweat the crime all that much. He'd endured far worse in Afghanistan, not that he spoke of it much. Getting him to give up the fast lane for the quiet life along the ocean would be an impressive trick.

Mom had found a ray of light, though. She told me that after I had left for my first year of college, Dad lost a spring in his step. He was working too much, and it was time to slow down and enjoy more time with his daughters while they were still at home, looking at him like Superman. There's just something about dads and daughters, Mom told me. She considered that an open door and arranged a two-week vacation with their best friends, the Maris family, at the Blue Lady.

Mom knew how difficult even contemplating such a radical move would be for Dad, so she convened a family meeting while he was out. My sisters and I were down with the idea of living at the Blue Lady. It was explained to us that if we wanted Dad to understand how peaceful life could be on the ocean, we all had to do our part to get along and avoid making Dad wish he'd never had children. We agreed. Mom made my sisters pinky swear.

I liked the idea of the family living near the sea. I loved it there, loved the misty air and cool mornings, loved sleeping to the lullaby of the crashing waves. A young man my age should have loved the big city. I didn't. Not a fan of the noise and speed. I've never been much of an adventurer. Quiet and calm was my preference, inherited from my mom.

I was Dad's opposite in that way, but another crucial difference weighed on me that summer—he was content with the trajectory of his life, and I was not. Worse yet, it would outwardly appear I had no right to discontentment. My first year as a college student on a football scholarship had gone well. It was a Division II school, but it was still impressive to be sporting one's way through school, a rare thing. I had my dad's rugged good looks. I was six-foot-four and well-muscled. I played tight end and spent my freshman season as a starter. I was waving to the girls in the stands when I wasn't flattening safeties and catching passes. It should have been a dream, and there was plenty to enjoy. But on balance, I was dying inside and wanted out.

In my quiet moments, I realized how much I treasured quiet moments. I hated the dictatorial structure of athletics and couldn't comprehend the micromanaged regime of college life. When conversations with my dad opened the door, I would hint at these feelings. Dad said many sacrifices would be made if a guy wanted to live free. I figured freedom was worth the sacrifice.

Dad would support me eventually. I had no doubt of that. But if I didn't have a backup plan, I would get a long talk about the dangers of diving off the high board with no water in the pool. Life ain't exactly breathing down your neck at nineteen, but time is always burning.

When Dad and I visited a woodworker's shop—Dad wanted to surprise Mom with a custom-made dining set for their anniversary—the proprietor gave us a tour of his shop before bringing us to his office to discuss it. His shop was an oversized garage next to his house in the country. After taking in his life's tranquility, the exquisite furniture pieces in his display room, and the sweet aroma of freshly worked wood, I knew how I wanted my life to look.

That night, I went home and planned it out. I would attend trade school, learn the craft, and set up at the Blue Lady. I'd ask Dad to let me live there rent-free for one year to get going, and after that, I would pay my way. I was confident in this plan. There were details to arrange that I wasn't aware of. Dad got a charge out of working out details, so I figured I stood on solid ground.

Some insecurities plagued me. Leaving college meant overturning a big apple cart. Losing the scholarship wasn't a financial blow to my parents, but I know Dad loved being a man whose son was footballing his way through college to study chemistry. It was hard to predict how he would react. He might love the idea of me spending a modest amount of time training as a woodsman and setting up shop. Or he might consider it an indulgent waste.

Then came Mom's idea to overhaul our entire family life. I hadn't told her or anyone of my schemes. I feared my plan would derail hers. It did seem like a lot to spoon onto Dad's plate, so I felt I had no choice but to see how her idea fared before I put my own into motion. The odds of getting Dad to retire to scale down were slightly above nil, so I figured I was safe to propose my own deal.

So that's where I was that summer. Ready to take adult control of my life. My college anxiety gave me a stark awareness of the time's full gallop. There was still living the part of me who found rare comfort riding carefree in the back of the car while Dad's sure and steady hand took us safely to the Blue Lady.

Madison turned around as far as her seatbelt would allow and looked at me. Her big brown eyes bore right into you. I took off my headphones and waited.

"Are there sharks in front of our house?" she asked.

"Sure, there are sharks," I said. "But the ocean is so big sharks are like a fart bubble in the water."

They laughed, a sweet sound I would play over and over in my mind so I wouldn't forget.

"Don't worry about it," I said. "Sharks like girls with red hair, anyway."

"Nuh-uh," Madison said.

"Yuh-huh," I said. "Look it up!"

She spun around. "Mom! Do sharks like to eat redhead girls?"

"I'm not sure sharks can see in color," Mom said.

That was just the sort of answer Mom would give to a question like that, an ambiguous response allowing either party to be correct.

Sophia looked back at me. She tossed her long blonde hair over her shoulder and fixed me with her inherited green eyes.

"I read that if a shark comes at you to punch it in the nose. That's what I would do," she said.

"Not a bad idea," I said.

We turned off the highway. The entrance to our private access road was hard to see due to trees and tall grass. Just as Dad liked it. Further in, a locked gate blocked the way. I got out, unlocked the padlock, and swung the gate open. He pulled through. I secured the gate once more, and we entered the woods.

The dirt road wound through the trees, deliberately designed in a wavy pattern to keep cars and trucks from speeding through. It was late afternoon, and the shadows were long. The gently passing trees and foliage created a soporific strobe of light and shadow. My sisters watched intently through their respective windows.

"Have you ever seen a bear, Dad?" Madison asked.

"Never seen one," he answered.

He pointed to a small clearing to the left. "Look there, though, three deer!"

Everyone oohed and aahed at the sight. For city folk, seeing such pristine breathing beauty was a treat. We didn't stop. We drove on. To watch them for too long was to ache.

We saw no more wildlife as we twisted and turned the rest of the way. The road straightened for the final twenty yards or so. We came out of the woods to see the Blue Lady framed by the ocean and the tangerine brushstrokes of an oncoming sunset.

The grand silhouette of the old gal never ceased to take my breath away. She wasn't all that wide for a Victorian home, but she still had the wraparound porch and pointed tower everyone associated with the design. Her blue paint was faded, and a fresh coat was about two years past due. I made a mental note to offer my services as a housepainter to sweeten the deal when I suggested my plan to Dad.

A two-car garage sat to the right of the house. On the left was a small meadow. Beyond the edges of the property, the forest began and stretched out for acres in each direction. A space of gravel and grass sat in front of the house, forming a parking area. An old-fashioned stone retaining wall enclosed this area.

Dad parked in front of the garage and shut off the Navigator. I could tell he and Mom wanted to take a moment and catch their breath after the long drive, but my sisters piled out as soon as the engine died and ran past the house, making a beeline for the beach. Mom sighed and left to chase them.

"Wait for me!" she hollered as they all vanished between the garage and the house.

Dad chuckled as he and I made a more leisurely exit from the car. We stretched and studied the facade of the house. With his practical eye, Dad checked for any apparent damage since the last time we'd been there.

"Well, let's go check 'er out," he said.

We stepped inside to gloomy shadows and musty air. I turned on the light, which revealed old-school elegance frozen in time. A grand staircase wound upwards. Arched ceilings yawned overhead, dwarfing us with her splendor. She had a large dining room, a cozy family room, a huge kitchen, and a den. Exquisitely carved wood adorned the staircase and fireplace mantle. The color scheme was likewise from another era, with each color a dark version of itself--navy blue, burgundy, old gold, etc. Little nooks and alcoves rested here and there. I spent many a summer reading comic books in the niche that looked out to the ocean.

Dad smiled as he took it all in. That only lasted a moment before he was off, walking the halls and checking the rooms. We went upstairs and looked in the bathrooms and bedrooms.

After walking the house, Dad pronounced it good. They hired people to keep it cleaned and prepare it for our arrival. He'd never had a complaint about them.

We unloaded the Navigator. First, we brought in three locked gun cases. We took those to the dungeon basement. There, Dad unlocked a metal door. It opened to a large storage room with homemade wooden shelves stocked high and deep with canned and dry goods and giant jugs of water. A gun safe stood just inside the door. He unlocked it, and we moved three AR-15s from the cases to the safe.

One of the rifles was mine, a gift from Dad for my high school graduation. In the gun safe, along with a cache of ammo, were three Smith & Wesson .357 revolvers. Along with Dad and I, Mom was trained in their use.

Dad had been the only survivor of a firefight in Afghanistan. He held out with little ammo and no food or water for three days. She didn't know much more than that, and it's a wonder she learned that much. Dad had resolved never again to be caught off guard.

We locked up the emergency provisions and weapons and checked the outside of the house and the grounds. Dad declared all to be well. We finished unloading and settled on the deck to watch Mom and the girls frolicking in the water. We each had a beer. Dad let me drink at the Blue Lady as long as I wasn't stupid. That was his only rule regarding any risk-taking: Don't be stupid.

After emptying my beer, I took off my shoes and strolled down the deck, through the wild grass, and onto the sand. It was warm and delicate, where the water never reached. Twenty or so steps, and I was on the cool, wet softness where the high tide rocked and rolled.

My sisters ran up to me and insisted I swing them, carry them, and toss them into the water like skipping stones. They loved having a giant for a big brother. I enjoyed it, too. They squealed and laughed, and it still echoes through the memory.

Dad waved us in. That could only mean our guests had arrived. We jogged back to the house and made our way around to the front. There, we found a full-size van parked next to our Navigator. Piling out was the Maris family. Their kids, Sebastian and Lydia, were around the same age as my sisters. I had trouble keeping track of ages. Philip Maris was a professor. Unassuming and soft-spoken, he looked the part of an academic with his beard, glasses, and khaki pants at the beach house. He and Dad were college buddies, and the friendship had endured and grown through the years.

From the passenger side of the van came Mrs. Maris. She was in her mid-forties, the same as my parents. She was a thin woman and taller than average. Her body was fit and narrow in the hips, making her large chest stand out even more than usual. Mom, speaking freely in front of me now and then because I was one of the grown-ups, referred to her as "Boobs on a Stick," not out of jealousy.

Her deep dimples framed a wide smile with teeth that were uneven yet perfect in a way braces would have ruined. Her thick brown hair cascaded down her shoulders, cradling that lovely face. The color of her eyes perfectly matched her hair.

She had always been beautiful, stopping conversations whenever she entered a room. Her big laugh matched a freewheeling sense of humor. All my life, I liked her the most of all my parents' friends. I only understood why later.

I called her Mrs. Maris back then. After she became my wife, I called her Kimberly.

MAN IN THE MIDDLE

There's something about getting together with good friends, especially for a shared vacation. It raises the energy level. It's an item on the list of good things you don't appreciate until they're gone. Never again would I enjoy such a moment in the sun. We hugged and shook hands and slapped backs. It was obvious everyone needed this vacation.

I was the "middle guy." Not yet as seasoned as my parents and their friends, not that much older than the young kinds. Depending on the circumstance, I bounced between the kids' and adults' tables.

Sebastian Maris was fifteen then. He wore an NFL jersey, but he wasn't very athletic. He hammered me with questions about playing in college and telling me how he watched all my games. Nice kid. I wanted to blow him off. Sports talk made me uncomfortable since I had planned to quit. He grinned as he walked up to me. More than anyone I knew, he loved that I was a college football player.

"Hey, Colby! Did you really play against Nebraska? IN Nebraska?"

"I sure did."

"And you scored?"

"First touchdown of the game, yes."

And our last score of the day. They beat the hell out of us.

"Cool. Did you get some good blocks?"

"Not as good as usual. They're Division I, we're Division II. But hey, I lived to tell about it."

"Wow!"

He was in awe, and I loosened up a bit.

His sister, Lydia, and my sisters ran for the beach, which meant adults had to follow to supervise. The moms and dads exchanged looks.

"I'll go this time," Dad said. "You ladies can unload."

"That's a man's job," Mom said. "Kim and I will go."

"Oh? Why do you get to decide what a man's job is?" Philip asked.

"Women's prerogative," Kimberly said.

As she passed, she gave me a hello hug. Not a fake side hug, but a tight, straight-on hug that pressed her big chest against my big chest. If she took note of the harmonic convergence taking place, she didn't show it. She did squeeze my shoulder on her way past.

"Hey, kiddo! Gettin' big!" she said.

Hey, kiddo, gettin' big??? Boy, did that deflate my ego. Women lightly groped my biceps and shoulders all the time. I was used to that, but she still saw me as one of the kids, which bothered me.

"You wanna go to the beach?" Sebastian asked.

I was trapped—still one of the kids. I didn't want to mope, though. I wanted to impress Dad with my adult perspective and attitude.

It was magic hour on the beach when we came around. The women and the girls were in the water. Mom and Kimberly vainly told the girls not to splash them.

"Want to see who can run the longest?" I asked Sebastian.

"You'll win," he said. "But I want to see how long I can go."

We took off on a steady jog in the sweet spot, where the sand was the perfect mix of hard and soft. I kept a leisurely pace that wouldn't wear out Sebastian too quickly. When we got to the far end of the beach, where the tree line curved into the mouth of our small bay, we turned around and came back to the house and to the other side. That was all Sebastian could handle. He begged off to tease the girls.

He was a chubby kid. Watching him walk away, winded, gave me an unfamiliar surge of emotion. I just really liked the kid in that moment. He wanted to be a jock but didn't have the genes for it. That didn't mean he couldn't get there, but it would take some mentoring from someone knowledgeable and interested, neither of which described his bookish teacher father. I decided to offer my services to get him on an exercise program. We'd find out just how much he wanted it.

I stood alone for a moment, watching Mom and Kimberly chat. It looked like a serious conversation. No joining that. I looked up to the deck, where Dad and Philip stood, each with a longneck. They had finished unloading and now readied the gas grill. They probably spoke of proper searing times for the ribeyes or their stock portfolios, or the Republicans or the Democrats, or their golf handicaps, or any other sort of manly subject I knew nothing about.

It was logical to take my place at the grill as a man should, but I knew the conversation would turn toward my football season. That was the one manly thing I could talk about at length and the one thing I didn't want to talk about right now.

I decided to resume my jog. I was ripped and fit after a season of tenacious football workouts. I took off my shirt and dropped it on the beach. The wind was warm and gentle. I wanted to feel as much of it as I could.

The run felt good. It gave me something to do and not feel awkward about being alone. No one else could run with my endurance, so I was safely isolated with my thoughts.

Curiosity struck. I wondered how this beach had looked one hundred years ago, five hundred years ago. I only knew some of the area's history, other than that Blackjack Hill, bordering our property to the north, had once been a pirate hideaway, with the ruins of a hidden fortress deep in the trees.

Other than that, I knew little. Had battles been fought here? Ships run aground? How old were the trees? If I stepped into a time machine and returned to the dinosaur era, would anything look different?

Those answers were easy to look up, a privilege I took for granted, at least in those days. I was content to let the land remain a mystery. Besides, I liked the idea that it never changed, and it hurt nothing to continue believing it.

I passed Mom and Kimberly. They watched me as I passed. I knew they talked about me and could only wonder what they said. I wanted to know what Kimberly said, but it was doubtful she spoke lustfully of me to my mother. Such were the hilarious ramblings of my brain back then.

I was trying to impress her, and that's all there was to it. If Kimberly had had a daughter my own age, my attentions might have wandered in that direction. But Kimberly was the only attractive, unrelated woman there, so my 19-year-old affections centered upon her. She would have laughed me off then, anyway.

I was sober-minded enough, just enough, to know that if I just let my crush have some air and not make a fool of myself, all would return to normal. Back to college or not, I'd find a girl my age and do everything as my parents and grandparents had. I was just a young man ready to take his place among the grown men, and a beautiful woman is a beautiful woman. I was in a new place; she was more or less in the same place she'd been for years.

I had a girlfriend in high school and was almost seeing a girl in college before the end of the semester stepped on the seedling of a relationship we had going. That was the extent of my romantic history, but it had taught me that two people who get together always start as perfect strangers.

Dad and Philip came down and told us the grill was heating up, and it was time to wash up for dinner.

The meal was delicious. The steaks had been seared and cooked to medium-rare goodness. The conversation was agony.

"Think you'll make the NFL draft?" Sebastian asked.

"No. I doubt it."

"I'll bet you could!"

"Sebastian," Philip said.

"Sorry."

"It's okay," I said. "It's hard to get into the pros."

"What's your major, Colby?" Philip asked. "Do you have one?"

"Chemistry."

Philip nodded his approval. "What do you plan to do with that degree?"

"I'm thinking maybe testing water."

I kept my answers short, hoping people would get the hint and change the subject.

"Like for a utility or something?" Philip asked.

"Yeah."

I was thinking of oceanography when I made the decision. It was the original plan, not the current plan, but it gave me an answer.

"Oh, to be young and have your whole life before you," Kimberly said. "I know you'll be great at it!"

Kiddo!

"Why? Would you do things differently?" Philip asked her with mock offense.

"Of course not!" she said, kissing him.

"If you ever need help with a school paper or any academic questions, I'm your man," Philip said.

"Cool, thanks."

"I, for one, am glad to get out of the city for a while," Mom said.

Thank you, Mom.

"Oh, don't I know it!" Kimberly said. "I won't go downtown without Philip."

I glanced at Philip, all one hundred and sixty pounds of him. What would he do to protect Kimberly? I chastised myself for thinking like that.

"And don't get me started on the schools," Philip said. "I can't believe how the high schools have deteriorated. What I wouldn't give for kids putting gum under the desk. That's a worry I could handle."

Philip was in his first year teaching high school geometry. He'd been a prominent professor on his way up when he'd run afoul of the cancel culture mob. I never knew the details. Got a pronoun wrong or used a word that had just been added to the list of non-approved words that morning or whatever. He'd refused to apologize, which Dad respected madly, and he'd been fired. Now, he was teaching high school, their finances were tight, and they were close to downsizing their house. All of this I heard through Mom. Philip didn't give Dad many details, although Dad told him he would help in any way he could

"How are things downtown by your office, Leo?" Kimberly asked. "I hear there's a homeless encampment by your building."

I'm sure Mom put her up to asking it.

Dad shrugged. "It is what it is. Of course, I don't like it, but there's not much that can be done. Or should I say, will be done. All this crime could be stopped quickly, but there's no political will to do it, nor is there will on the part of the voters to elect someone who will stop it."

"You don't worry?" Kimberly asked.

"I should pay more attention to it, I suppose," Dad said. "But I've seen worse. Look, people have the city they voted for. I don't see it getting better on its own. There will be a correction at some point. It will come from the outside and will do so in a way we won't miss."

"That sounds ominous," Philip said.

"Just remember to look alive when it comes," Dad said.

Mom glanced at the kids and back to Dad, who got the hint.

"Not to worry, though," he said. "We must live with faith and confidence that tomorrow will be a better day."

"Not if the UFOs land," Sebastian said.

Everyone looked at him.

"You haven't heard about them?" he asked.

"Sebastian," Philip said precisely as he had before.

"What? They flew over Seattle, you know. Also London and Paris and all over."

"It's a silly subject," Philip said.

"I've heard about that," Dad said with a smile. "What do you think they are, Sebastian?"

"They're from Sirius," he said.

"Seriously?" Philip asked.

"Fine, never mind."

Everyone was quiet.

"There's always something flying around, Honey," Kimberly said. "It happens so often that I don't pay much attention to it anymore. Nothing ever happens. They fly around with their weird lights and leave. Big whoop."

"Experimental military craft, obviously," Philip said.

None of this made Sebastian feel any better. Strange military planes were pretty cool but couldn't compete with sleek spaceships from Sirius. Sebastian and all the other kids knew that their interests did not jive with those of the grown-ups at the table. Everyone has to come to that realization sooner or later. The grown-up conversations moved on to more mundane things, and the kids fell to talking and laughing about whatever jokes and fads they kept up with.

Sebastian was right. There were absolutely UFOs being spotted over cities across the world. Kimberly was also correct in that such sightings always seem to flare up, get some attention, and fade away with nothing happening. We should have asked Sebastian what he thought should be done if aliens decided it was time to conquer planet Earth.

The regular come-and-go pattern that UFOs usually took was about to be upended. Although we didn't know it, we had one more night of peace in an ordinary world.

The rest of the night was board games and movies. The grown-ups went for a romantic moonlight stroll on the beach to watch the tide go out. I had been distracted while packing and hadn't brought anything for downtime. I found myself sitting through two animated movies, both of which were better than I had feared, but by the end, I had to tap out and do something else.

The shelves were stacked with paperbacks from vacations of bygone eras. I picked up a Michael Crichton book, said good night, and went to my room. It was a great read. I figured it would put me to sleep fast enough, but it kept me up late.

I'm pondering a lot of minutia here, but after all these years, I still cling to memories of those final hours and minutes. I wouldn't change anything if I had a time machine. Maybe it's best to live life and let it end when it will.

My room was in the tower of the house. I staked that claim the first time my parents brought me there. My window faced west. It had a beautiful view of the sea. It was the only place I ever took the time to sit and stare. The sea was so hypnotic. I asked nothing of it. I didn't long for answers or guidance or expect it to speak to me. I just liked being with it.

Since the window faced west, I didn't get direct sunlight through my windows until the afternoon of the next day. Using an alarm clock on vacation seemed like a horrible thing to do. So, by the time I was awake and moving about for the day, everyone else had already finished breakfast and planned their day.

Mom and Dad went into the nearby village to pick up some groceries and other household and maintenance stuff. Philip went with them. Kimberly planned to take the kids on a hike up Blackjack Hill.

I never missed a chance to see the ruins of the old pirate fortress. Legend said there was still gold and jewels to be found. The hill was beyond our property line, but ever since my great-grandfather, our family had worn down several hiking paths through the woods to the top of the peak. If my ancestors ever found the pirate treasure, they kept it for themselves and never told anyone. Everyone had been drilled on the importance of staying on the path and not wandering off into the trees.

Dad insisted I take a revolver and bear spray with me. Nobody had ever encountered a bear, but there was a first time for everything, and you never knew what kind of human wildlife might slither out from under a rock.

The path was steep and uneven. Trees reached overhead in a sinister grasp, darkening the woods. The wind tickled the leaves, making it sound like great and small creatures followed us, invisible in the green.

Sophia and Madison got nervous after one too many noises. They held my hand. Soon, I had Madison hugging my thigh. It wasn't easy to walk. I stopped and squatted low.

"All right, hop on," I said.

Both girls cheered and crawled onto my back. I stood up and kept walking. I turned around to make sure Kimberly and her kids were following. Lydia was likewise skittish and wanted a ride. I was about to make room for a third.

"I'll carry you, Lydia," Sebastian said.

She hopped on his back. He lumbered a bit but carried her on like a champ. Kimberly smiled at us.

"I guess I get a free walk!" she said.

She passed us. The Maris family had been up here with us many times. She knew the way.

We broke through the tree line and crested the top of the hill. I walked to the edge for the excellent view. The girls stayed on my back and tightened their grip near the precipice. Lydia jumped down from Sebastian. Kimberly kept her kids further back.

"Colby, when will I be too old for you to carry us?" Madison asked.

"Never."

"What about when I'm thirty," she asked. "I'll be too heavy then, right?"

"You'll never be too heavy for me to carry."

"What if I'm on a reality show because I'm so fat? How about then?" Madison asked.

"Still no problem."

"What would you do if a bear came at us?" Sophia asked.

"I'd pick him up and toss him over the edge, right into the ocean."

We were quiet for a moment as we watched the waves crash in. They seemed to move in slow motion.

"Colby, will you always look out for us?" Sophia asked.

"Of course," I said. "I'll watch out for you for the next hundred years."

Mom and Dad

I couldn't have known it then, but those silent moments at the summit of Blackjack Hill would be the last time I knew total peace. I sensed Kimberly felt it, too. Even the kids seemed to know. They stood quietly, staring out at the vast ocean below as if they knew we had entered a moment that shouldn't be interrupted.

Who could speak standing before such a perfect painting? It stretched into infinity in all directions. The lazy waves, cobalt sky, puffy clouds, and embracing wind answered all questions and defied all observation. Sea mist whirled and twirled its way up the cliffside, sighing and caressing, filling our senses with ancient ties to the first of humanity to see it all.

One could only stand in the glow for so long before the sensation up and left you. Valid for so many things. Kimberly and I turned away to leave at the same time. The kids immediately followed. Their brains and jaws poured out dozens of questions. We did our best to sound smart.

We led the kids back down the descending return path. Dad insisted people return the way we came, as the descending path took hikers deeper into the woods. Since I was with them and carried mace and a pistol, I figured Dad wouldn't mind. Sebastian led the way down into the woods.

When kids passed into the trees, Kimberly touched my shoulder and pointed at the sky. "Look at that!" she whispered.

The UFOs were high and far away. They darted around, zig-zagging far beyond what a human pilot could endure. I'd seen UFOs on TV before, almost to the point of boredom, but this was my first sighting. No one could have told me it was reflections or swamp gas. As it would anyone, it gave me a sense that something otherworldly had revealed itself.

For a few minutes, they moved randomly, as if unaware of each other and searching for direction. In seconds, they stabilized and began to coast with speed and purpose, crisscrossing the sky in an organized grid pattern that was unsettling in its deliberateness. The formation came over us, about two thousand feet up. They were all the same size—almost as big as a hot air balloon. They were perfectly round and made of a silver-like metal with an iridescent reflection.

Kimberly and I slowly looked down from the sky and at each other. She took a step closer to me. Did she feel safer near me? I went with that assumption because I liked the idea.

"Weird," she said.

We continued and caught up with the kids. The UFOs were lost to us as we passed under the vast canopy of leaves. Sebastian had set a hearty pace for the walk back.

I was disturbed by the sighting but felt no urgent sense of danger. Not yet. There was an ongoing UFO "flap" in those days. It had happened a couple of times in my memory. I'm sure older generations like Kimberly's and my parents had seen such things many times. Dad always brushed it off as the military testing secret technology and was probably egging on the UFO bunk on their own. If everyone's squawking about UFOs, nobody's wondering where their tax dollars are going and will even see the military as the heroes should things go cross-eyed. UFOs had come and gone to varying degrees of fanfare, and there was no reason to think this time would be any different. We walked on.

No wildlife appeared to us that day. The kids were disappointed. It was unusual not to even see a deer off in the thicker parts of the woods. I wondered if the UFOs triggered some survival instinct that prompted them to get lost.

The path took us past a blind curve to a clearing in a hollow. It was a vast, flat meadow in the middle of the woods. After the cool air of the trees, it got hot again when you entered the clearing. The ground sloped up on one end, and there was an indentation that curved into its wall. Dad thought it was an old cave filled in God knows how many years ago. I had begged Dad to dig it out and see for sure. He said we didn't own the land. I argued that nobody would notice. He said, "We'll see," which meant it never happened. Now I had the girls working on him. Daughters are far more persuasive to Dads than sons.

We let Sebastian and the girls have some fun in the clearing. It was a natural playground. There were ancient tree trunks and fallen trees. The crumbling remnants of a stone wall surrounding the area gave the kids something to crawl on. Some of my favorite memories took place there. I showed them how to extend the wall with fallen branches. Kimberly pretended to be a captured maiden who needed rescuing. I was the lousy pirate. Sebastian, Lydia, Madison, and Sophia were the Lost Kids, as they called themselves, who saved the day.

Kimberly and I tired out and sat on the old stones to watch the kids. The kids squealed and played in their own world, leaving me with Kimberly in ours. We watched them for a few minutes, then she turned to me, smiling.

"How's school?" she asked.

I didn't want to lie to her. I didn't know why at the time.

"I'm thinking of quitting," I said.

"Oh," she said, staying calm.

She worked hard not to say anything negative. Very sweet of her.

"Well, there are other paths in life," she said. "Have you thought about other paths?"

"I'm thinking about building furniture."

"Really? How awesome!" she said. "Well, let me know when you're up and running. I need a new bureau."

She didn't judge and was all-in on my new idea. She was still Mrs. Maris but had been promoted to the coolest grown-up I knew.

"I haven't told Dad," I said.

She hadn't mentioned my parents' reaction, which was another plus in her favor. She nodded as she considered that.

"Well, your Dad's understanding. He'll support you. You'll see."

After all that epic battling, I could tell Kimberly was tiring. Even the kids looked out of gas, so we started home. By the time we came out of the woods and onto our beach. Madison was dead asleep in my arms. It was lunchtime, and everyone was ready for a sandwich.

We went onto the deck and heard car doors shutting. Mom, Dad, and Philip were back from their shopping trip. They had done more shopping than we realized. Dad had hooked up the small trailer. It was loaded with bags of concrete, posts, and rolls of chain link fencing. There were also several coils of razor wire. The good vibes of our hike were gone.

Dad saw our looks.

"Just a precaution," he said. "At the village, we found out things are going south in Seattle."

"Going south, how?" Kimberly asked.

"Oh, some UFO crap getting people panicked," Philip said.

"I came back for the trailer, and we went to the Home Depot in the village," Dad said. "We need to seal off the property."

That sounded ominous.

"You think there's an alien invasion coming?" I asked.

"No," he said. "But it doesn't matter what I believe. Nutjobs in the city believe it, and they're fleeing to the country in droves."

"There are reports of homes in the country getting ransacked," Philip said.

"Who knows if they're really scared or just looking for an excuse to loot and go crazy," Mom said.

"Either way, we need to shore things up," Dad said.

The property was already fenced off in the back. It was a nice wrought-iron fence that kept the animals out and kept youngsters from wandering off into the ocean. I wondered what he had in mind. He read my thoughts.

"I want to create a perimeter fence around the front here," he said.

"Hey, kids, let's get in our suits and hit the water. What do you say?" Kimberly said.

Sebastian and Sophia looked worried and knew Kimberly was trying to distract them. But it was the age where you know grown-ups will take care of whatever needs taking care of.

Mom went with Kimberly. I helped Dad and Philip unstrap the load. Their manner was severe but not overly worried.

"Dad, is it bad? Is there trouble coming?"

"I don't know, Son. But the more we're prepared, the better it will be. I've been wanting to seal off the front of this property for a long time."

Going from contentment to anxiety so fast left me paralyzed for the moment. Dad gave me instructions. Getting busy with my hands calmed my mind. Dad said I got to dig the holes since I was the biggest. I ran to the shed, got the post-hole digger, and punched open the ground where Dad had marked it. Dad and Philip followed behind me, sinking poles in concrete.

By mid-afternoon, the poles were up. We had a quick snack while watching everyone else swim. After that, we returned to work, unrolling the chain link fencing and attaching it to the poles. Philip took a roll of razor wire and went to top off the backyard fencing.

Dad and I worked in silence for a few minutes. I got the hang of it, and we worked quickly, four hands of the same mind. We finished the fence, and Dad talked me through creating a double-door gate. It was mid-afternoon when we started topping the fence with razor wire. Of course, I nicked myself a time or two.

Something about the sight of that wire got to me. The vacation getaway now appeared as a sinister compound from all the post-apocalyptic thrillers I like to watch.

"What do you think will happen?" I asked.

"Oh, I think it will blow over before it gets too bad," he said. "When we're talking about the people in charge, there's certain kinds of unrest they like, certain kinds they don't."

"What's that mean?"

"What it means is, if the riots get put down quickly, they are a threat to power. If things continue, then the unrest is useful."

"What if things are really bad this time?"

"You mean if the aliens come?"

"Well, yeah, why not?"

"Anything's possible, I guess," he said. "If it's aliens and they have death phasers, well, there's nothing we can do about that, so no sense fretting over it. It's people I'm worried about."

"You think they'll get this far south?"

"The access road is so hidden it's hard to see if you don't know it's there. Honestly, I think things will be okay," he said. "This isn't about living in fear, Son, it's about being ready, raising our level of awareness."

"Okay, cool."

"You remember the combinations to the storage room and gun safe?"

I recited them. He nodded, and we returned to working quietly for a few minutes. I had planned to let Mom make her pitch to Dad before burdening him with my plans. Considering the unrest back home and around other big cities, I figured she had all the ammunition she could need, so I went for it.

"I've been thinking about college," I said.

"Thinking how?" he asked, not looking up.

"Thinking about leaving, to be honest."

Now, I had his full attention.

"What about the team? You're a starter. All-conference alternate."

"I know. Coach won't be happy."

"And the scholarship?"

My scholarship was sure to be renewed, considering how well I played. Dad could afford to send me anywhere, but that wasn't the point. Dad hated waste, especially the rich-kid-don't-need-to-care type of waste.

"It's just not what I want to do."

"What is it you want to do?"

There was tension in his voice like he worried I would get in a Chevy Van, cruise America, pick up long-legged Sallys, and find myself.

"Remember that woodworker we visited last year?"

Dad put it all together right away. "You want to be a woodsman? Far out."

I'd never heard him say "far out" before. Before he could question me, I laid out my plan as described earlier. I kept working on the razor wire while I talked. He stood back and listened. I finished my pitch and waited for his reaction. He returned his attention to the wire.

"Sounds like a solid plan," he said. "I think you'll do great at it."

"Really?"

"Sure. Now is the time to take charge of your destiny. A man has a right to do so. I'll always love you and support you. I know your mom would say the same."

I thought I would cry. No argument. No badgering. Just confident acceptance. What more did any son want to hear?

"Just make sure you tell your coach immediately," he said. "You'll have to tend to all the details of it, big shot."

He winked.

"Your grandfather would have liked to see me join the family law firm, but he never pressed me on it when I chose a different path," he said. "You need to set up your own kingdom."

Kingdom, I liked that.

"I've been set up doing what I want to do for many years now," he said. "There aren't any mountains left for me to climb. Maybe I need to think about what comes next. I know your Mom wants me to retire. She tries to give me small hints, but she's about as subtle as a train wreck."

"You think you might?" I asked, thinking about Mom's reaction.

"Well, it's too soon to retire, which means I'm young enough to try something new. What do you think? What should my final act be?"

"You could fix up houses so they're ready for the end of the world."

He thought about that. "I just might."

I was spent after helping with the fence and the relief of telling Dad about my plans to leave college and football. I felt guilty for assuming he would bust my chops over it. Sometimes, parents surprise you. Seeing his sense of control and habit of thinking things through before acting or speaking, was good.

It was only the first day. I hoped the rest of the vacation would go well now that my mind was clear. I took a nap.

Dinner was fun but uneventful. The couples were especially cuddlesome and affectionate. Sebastian teased the girls. They gave it right back to him. Conversation ebbed and flowed, with long, comfortable silences only old friends can enjoy. After dinner dishes were cleared, we agreed to reconvene for board games after the grown-ups had their after-dinner cocktails.

Since I was yet to be part of that drinking club, I volunteered to help the kids with the dishes. When that was done, I walked out to the beach. The sun was down, but the last swishes of color gave the water, the sand, and all of us the cinematic glow of an eighties movie.

The Marises stood together, arm and arm, closed off from the world and watching the horizon. I looked further down the beach and saw Mom. She was alone. I'd passed Dad checking razor wire on my way out. She didn't see me at first.

I often think of Mom as I saw her barefoot on the sand that night. She stood in her beach dress, watching the sea, lost in her thoughts, her own world. Her green eyes and cropped blonde hair glistened in the fading light. Her full lips were bent in a slight, contented smile. It aches to conjure that image, wondering what she would have been like in older age, imagining her delighted laughter as her future grandchildren ran to her.

She sensed my presence and smiled. She waited and let me come to her. I wanted to gather her in a big hug, since I felt waves of affection for all she had done for me.

"Hey," she said.

It was nice to hear the soft tones of her natural voice, rather than the "mom" voice I'd elicited from her throughout my childhood.

"Hey," I said.

We stood quietly for a few minutes, a silence that knew someone had something to say.

"Your father told me about your change in direction," she said.

She knew all about it. I'd confided in her and sought her advice. It was how things worked with my parents. I'd run it by Mom first, and she would make sure I had my ducks in a row before approaching Dad with it.

"He seemed okay with it," I said.

"He is," she said. "Are you sure you're quitting football?"

"I think so."

"You think so?"

"No, I'm sure. I'm done. I know what I want to do now."

"Good."

"How about you?" I asked. "Are you okay with it?"

"Are you kidding? I hate watching you play football!"

That wasn't a huge surprise, but I didn't realize she was so emphatic.

"You did well, but all I saw were those boys getting hurt," she said. "Besides, you need to get practiced up, because I have a lot of furniture I want you to build!"

"I'll do that," I said. "You're not mad? I kinda jumped the gun before you could talk to Dad about retiring."

She waved that off. "Oh, don't worry about that. After this latest nonsense in the city, convincing him might not be hard."

"You think this is worse than usual?"

She shrugged and shook her head simultaneously—one of her signature moves.

"I'm too sensitive to it to be objective," she said. "I would just like to get out. I'm an old soul. The kind that wants to die an old lady in my sleep!"

Dad came out from his chores with the fence. I hugged Mom and went for an evening run so they could have some time together.

THE BEAM

Dad woke me early the following day and told me to get dressed and come down. He said to be careful not to wake the kids. I came downstairs, and he led me out to the beach. We found Mom and the Marises in their pajamas, staring at the sky, watching the UFOs fly about in the same pattern.

Kimberly saw me first.

"The same ones we saw yesterday," she said.

"Only a lot closer," I said.

"Where did you see them?" Dad asked.

I told him how we saw them on Blackjack Hill and about their strange movements.

"They're talking about them on the news," Dad said.

We had spotty internet service in those days and no cable. Living rustic (a little, not too much) was part of the point of having an isolated house by the sea. We had an antenna that picked up a couple of big-city stations; otherwise, we had to bring DVDs if we wanted to watch something.

"What are they saying?" Mom asked.

"They're causing a panic," Dad said.

"What are those things doing that would cause a panic?" Philip asked, alarm in his voice.

He started thumbing away on his smartphone.

"No coverage?" he asked.

"Spotty coverage. The idea is to get away from technology," Dad said.

"Understandable," Philip said, hiding his frustration out of respect for Dad.

"We can keep an eye on the local news," Dad said. "But we need to stay alert on our own. Only a fool would trust only what they're told."

"Did the news say anything else about them?" Mom asked.

Dad acted as if he didn't want to share this part. "The UFO attacks have caused looting and riots. The roads out of Seattle are jammed. Everyone's trying to escape. Roving gangs are looting houses up and down the highway not far from here. They may find us."

"UFO attacks?" Mom asked.

"I'm curious how these UFOs are attacking," Philip said. "Did we wake up in a disaster movie? Really?"

"Some sort of weapon is firing on the city," Dad said. "Not just Seattle. Cities all over the world."

"Oh my God," Kimberly said.

I felt nauseous. It was turning out to be a bad movie.

"We need to finish securing the house," Dad said. "It won't just be panicked people trying to break in; they will be bad enough. There's going to be bad people taking advantage of the situation."

"Over this?" Philip asked.

"We don't punish violent crime anymore, Philip," Dad said. "The groundwork for this unrest has been laid, and now we must deal with it."

The first thing Dad did was put everyone through a gun safety course. Everyone fired into an earthen berm bordering the southern end of the property. The women took revolvers. The rest of us slung rifles over our shoulders.

Next, we placed security bars across the doors and covered the windows with custom wood shutters. Dad had made the shutters himself. They were two layers of wood with a section of sheet metal sandwiched between them, making them bulletproof. The security bars and shutters were painted to perfectly match the interior paint of the rooms, making them more out of sight and out of mind.

Growing up, I had often helped Dad while he made things like this. I helped him stock the storage room and take inventory. I used to chuckle and shake my head at Dad's "prepper nonsense." I wouldn't have lived without it, as it turns out. Part of my amusement at his strident readiness was a subconscious desire that it would never be needed. As a college boy and no longer a kid, I still wanted Dad to tell me everything would be okay.

"Do we need to be carrying these guns?" I asked.

"I hope not, Son. Let me put it this way," he said. "Let's say it takes three minutes, give or take, to get down to the storage room, get into the gun safe, get the rifle, lock and load, and get back upstairs and outside in time to deal with any threat. And let's say it takes the same amount of time to return the rifle to the safe after carrying it and not needing it. Which three minutes is gonna take longer? Rushing down to get it when you need it and don't have it? Or taking your time to put it back after a false alarm?"

I had no answer, so I kept the rifle over my shoulder and asked no more dumb questions until the house was secure. We finished everything just in time to see the kids come down for a late breakfast. It took them about two seconds to notice that all the grown-ups had guns.

"Cool!" Sebastian said. "Can I have a gun, too?"

"Sorry, kid," Philip said.

"Is everything okay, Daddy?" Sophia asked.

Dad glanced around at the other grown-ups. One by one, he looked them in the eye. All of them nodded. It was time to be honest with the kids.

"Well, gang, you need to know that there's trouble in the city," he said. "But we've done everything we can to make this house and the yard and the beach and everything as safe as it can be."

"Are people going to try to hurt us?" Madison asked.

"I don't know, Sweetie," Dad said. "But we're all here to protect you. And it's very important that you listen to us and do exactly what we say, when we say it. Okay? Do you all want to be part of the home defense team?"

That last question had such halftime-speech gusto that the kids cheered their agreement. The rest of us smiled for the first time that morning. We enjoyed a moment of optimism as we joined the kids for breakfast.

The first attack came around mid-afternoon. Not from aliens, but humans. They arrived not in a metal flying sphere but in one of those souped-up trucks with oversized tires and mounted lights. The scattered news reports we've been following told us that marauders were out. During press conferences, reporters asked civil authorities if this was organized crime in any way or just lone wolves out taking advantage of opportunities. The mayor and police officials adamantly denied any organization to the unfolding chaos. I didn't need Dad to tell me that was a garbage lie. When I looked at him, he was already shaking his head, staring at the floor.

"My ass," he said.

Soon after everyone had showered and dressed, we heard the first gunshots in the distance. We listened to the rumble of loud engines. Screams rang out occasionally, sometimes solitary, sometimes in groups. As frightening as the UFOs had become, our immediate danger was human evil.

Dad told Kimberly and Mom to take the children down to the storage room and lock the door. If anyone came through, either crashing the door or unlocking it with the key, and it wasn't one of the three of us. They were to shoot them without hesitation.

They scrambled downstairs. When they were gone, Dad stood before Philip and me.

"Philip, you get upstairs to your bedroom. Keep the lights off and find a spot around the curtain. Keep the rifle aimed at the front gate, safety off.

"Colby, you open that front shutter a few inches. Stay as out of the way as you can and still be able to see outside. Same thing for you—aim at the gate—safety off.

"Keep your fingers off the trigger until it's time to fire. I'll find a spot on the side of the house. Colby, you do the talking. It's very simple:

you tell them we aren't taking visitors, and that they are to turn back immediately. If they try to break in, they will be fired upon."

"What if they argue? What if they don't listen?" I asked.

"You just keep repeating what I told you," Dad said. "Don't shoot until I do. I'll fire a warning shot. If it looks like they're gonna crash the gate, I'll fire at them directly. When that happens, both of you open up. Hear me and hear me well, gentlemen, when you shoot, you don't shoot to hurt; you shoot to kill. Do you understand?"

We both nodded. I had trouble stopping my limbs from shaking. Never had I been so afraid. The only thing keeping me sane was Dad's focused energy.

"I can't emphasize enough how serious this is," Dad said. "This is our families' safety we're talking about. You don't want to think about what they'll do with our women if they take them."

"What if they're not looters?" I asked.

"If it's a misunderstanding, they'll apologize and turn around," Dad said. "Now, let's get to our positions."

This happened quickly as we heard the truck roar, winding its way along the private road to the house. Thank God great-grandpa had thought to build the road this way.

Philip ran upstairs to his room, white as a goal line. Dad watched me prop the shutter open and take my place. He gave me a few suggestions to ensure I was as safe as possible, and then he ran toward the rear of the house.

"I'll be on the north side," he said as he left.

I was on my own then, sick to my stomach with fear and thinking only about how only yesterday I stood at the top of Blackjack Hill with

Kimberly, and all seemed perfect. But there was no time to reminisce. The big brown monster truck appeared at the entrance to the property. Besides the driver, a man in the passenger seat had his arm out the window, holding an AR-15 rifle similar to ours. Two other men stood in the truck's bed, also brandishing rifles. All were big, bearded men.

They paused for a moment, studying the house. The two men in the truck bed leaned over to talk to the men in the cab. By their hand gestures, it was apparent they meant to ram the gate. It would be easy to do. The chain-link fence would offer no resistance to the truck that size.

I wondered when I was supposed to say my line. The truck suddenly revved loudly and flattened the gate's two halves, bringing down part of the attached fence. They stopped almost immediately. One of the men in the truck bed fired his rifle into the air.

"Everybody out!" he yelled.

I was never an actor, but I knew a cue when I heard it. I ducked away from the slit in the window.

"We are not taking any visitors! Turn back immediately! If you come any closer, you'll be fired upon!"

The men in the truck bed crouched down. Those in the cab shrunk down in their seats. They glanced over the dashboard, quickly scanning the house, looking for a rifle in a window. I hoped Philip was well-hidden.

I heard gunfire and damn near jumped out of my pants. I overcame my terror and looked out the window to see the men in the truck taking cover. Dad had fired his warning shots. Once they realized the shots were meant to warn and not to harm, they opened fire on the house. Three bullets struck the shutter I had propped open.

I collapsed on the floor, clutching my rifle, sweating and shaking. More shots rang out, this time coming from upstairs and the side of the house. This meant Dad and Philip had joined the gunfight. I was clear-headed enough to know that I didn't want to explain myself to Dad when he asked why I hid on the floor and did nothing.

I pointed my rifle out the window, aimed at the truck, and fired. The man in the passenger seat of the truck was bloodied and still. Only one man now stood in the truck bed. The driver fired out his window with an automatic pistol. The last man standing in the truck bed did his best to hide, but I saw him lighting a Molotov cocktail.

The three of us concentrated our fire on the man and took him out quickly. We shattered his jar of fuel as he lit it. He screamed as he went up in flames. The burning fuel poured over the truck's roof, windshield, and hood. The driver panicked, put the truck in reverse, and recklessly spun backward from the parking area. They barreled out of sight. Seconds later, we heard the truck crash and saw smoke coming from the road.

I never learned if I had killed any of them. We regrouped in the living room. None of us were hurt. Dad was grim and determined. Philip and I were still high on adrenaline but uncertain what to think. Dad made it clear we had done what needed to be done, that the cost of inaction then or in the future would mean the life or death of all of us.

When Dad felt enough time had passed, we walked to the truck to make sure it was over. We followed Dad's lead. I wondered if this was what it had been like for him in Afghanistan. Had he endured stress and terror at this level daily? It was a wonder he could still function at all. I had played a double-overtime game in one-hundred-degree heat and wasn't as exhausted as I was then.

We found the four men dead. The smoldering truck was charred black. Their weapons were ruined. Dad had us take them anyway. He decided against burying the bodies or moving the truck. He figured it would be a suitable warning to anyone with similar ideas.

By dinnertime, everyone's nerves had calmed about as much as they could have. Kimberly could barely believe Philip had participated in a gunfight. He seemed pleased, thinking she was impressed. It felt good to have scored a win, but no one knew what this meant for the future. Would there be more? How many? Lots of bad scenarios passed through my imagination and wouldn't leave.

There was no hiding anything from the kids at that point. They knew the everyday world, as they had come to know it, was no more. Bad things were happening. Bad people were doing bad things. They didn't give into despair, though, because at their age, they still believed the grown-ups would see everyone through, that things could go back to the way they once were when things made sense to them. I ate silently, realizing that no matter how long we lived, there was no going back. There was only going through.

After dinner, the craft and their calculated patterns attacked our house. We huddled inside upon learning of what the news called The Beam, some death ray decimating city populations worldwide. We assumed that wood, stone, and steel would protect us from the Beam's effects, at least for a while. What, exactly, the Beam was doing was unknown.

We heard it and felt its vibration as it approached. As scary as the gunmen were, their weapons, big truck, and Molotov cocktails were nothing compared to the mind-numbing fear the oncoming alien beam brought.

Dad and I watched it draw near from the ocean. From underneath a craft, it fanned out until it reached the water. Only the distorted air made it visible. It swept across the water. Millions of droplets leaped into the air like a giant guitar string had been snapped beneath the surface. It came ashore and scattered sand. Philip joined us. He looked confused.

"That's it?" Philip asked. "If that's the extent of it, we should count ourselves lucky."

"Maybe they're using something else in the cities," Mom said.

"Let's just stay inside," Dad said.

The craft and its beam was almost to the house.

"Everyone away from the windows," Dad said.

We settled on chairs and sofas in the living room. The kids curled up on their parents' laps. Madison sat with me. We waited for whatever was going to happen.

The beam hit the house, shaking the walls and rattling the windows with the force of a high wind. We saw each other through a funhouse lens as it came through the house. Everyone gasped. The kids even giggled as the beam passed through us. Our hair stood on end, and our stomachs got the butterflies. I thought I might piss my pants. It only took seconds for that strange sensation to sweep through.

When it was over, we looked at each other, looking to make sure everyone was all right. Parents asked if the kids were okay. The kids thought it was funny, considering we were tickled more than anything else.

"Everyone feeling all right?" Dad asked.

There were no injuries, headaches, nosebleeds, or anything else to indicate people were hurt.

Dad seemed to relax for the first time in a long time. "I think you're right, Philip. Maybe we are lucky."

Philip stretched and yawned. He didn't just sort of yawn. He nearly dislocated his jaw. He stood and stretched and yawned a second time. He rubbed his eyes and briefly lost his balance. Kimberly watched him, concerned and amused.

"What's wrong, hon?" she asked.

Philip yawned again. "I'm so damn tired all of a sudden."

"Now? Just like that?" she asked.

Philip hobbled toward the stairs and slowly made his way up.

"Just for a bit," he said. "Don't let me sleep for more than an hour."

Everyone stared at the empty staircase when he was gone. It should have been evident that Phil's sudden fatigue was related to the beam that had just passed through us. Since the beam didn't match our preconceived notions, we dismissed it. Even if we had known there was a connection, we'd have only discovered the horrible truth sooner.

Eternal Sleep

Silence lingered after Philip went up for his nap. We needed time to catch our breath because the last few seconds had been so bizarre that nobody knew what to say or do.

"It felt like somebody was tickling my guts," Madison said.

Dad chuckled. "Yeah, I know what you mean. Felt like that to me, too."

"I know everyone keeps asking this," Mom said. "But is that it? This can't be what's killing people in the cities."

"Maybe we're not being told the truth about what's happening in the cities," Kimberly said.

"We have firsthand evidence of the unrest out there smoking in the woods," Dad said.

"What do you mean, Daddy?" Sophie asked.

The grown-ups exchanged a look. I had seen that look many times—a look that said the discussion was not for little ears and that the little ears must be given something else to do.

Dad announced it was time for the kids to watch a movie in the family room. They were disappointed, as I had been each time that line had been run on me, but Dad sweetened the deal by telling them they could watch an R-rated movie as long as it passed parental veto.

It was a powerful incentive and had the desired effect.

With the kids gone, I tried to remember any movie or book that would give me a leaping-off point to offer some speculation that made sense. I didn't read any more nonfiction than my college classes required. Pop culture was my only reference.

"All I think this tells us is that events are still unfolding," Dad said. "I don't think we have any other choice but to wait and see what else happens."

"I don't know how much more stress I can take," Mom said. "Is there any way we can get some real information? Maybe the news has something new."

Dad turned on the TV. He clicked around until he found a channel that came in clear enough to understand. It was primarily shots of buildings burning and people running in the streets.

"You can almost feel the glee these news people are feeling," he said. "Suffering means ratings."

"Leo, shush," Mom said. "Now's not the time."

A pretty talking head appeared on the screen with a graphic indicating the Federal Emergency Management Agency provided her talking points. It wasn't much different from emergencies in the past — stay at home, listen to instructions from civil authorities, check in on neighbors, the elderly, and shut-ins, but there were a couple of frightening wrinkles thrown in toward the end.

The early reports of people getting killed were accurate. Film clips aired of bodies being loaded onto flatbed trucks. Survivors screamed and wailed along the sidewalks and streets. Ambulances, hearses, and police cars were everywhere. The talking head babe grimly told her viewers that federal and state authorities were cooperating to create makeshift morgues for people to bring their dead.

Then came the tidbit that changed everything. She told us if the "victim" could not be rousted from sleep after 15 minutes and had no pulse or signs of breathing, they were to call the emergency number on the screen and arrange to bring the victim to a makeshift clinic/morgue so their life signs could be officially evaluated. If the person was dead, then by presidential executive order, the dead were to be left at the medical centers for disposal by the military.

"You gotta be kidding me," Dad said.

The newscaster moved on to more fearful clips.

"Who would leave their loved ones to be tossed into a pit by the military?" he asked.

"There must be so many dead they don't have a choice," I said.

It was the first time I had spoken since the wave went through. I could barely croak the words out. I went to get a drink of water.

"What did she mean by 'rousted from sleep?'" Kimberly asked.

"We must have missed some earlier context," Mom said. "I think we should keep the news on constantly from now on."

I filled a glass of water and heard Dad putting it together from the kitchen.

"I guess the logical assumption right now is that the beam puts people to sleep so they never wake up," he said.

I returned from the kitchen to find Dad, Mom, and Kimberly with horrible looks on their faces. Kimberly pointed upstairs with a shaking hand.

"Philip went up there to nap almost twenty minutes ago," she said. "H-he got tired almost immediately after that beam went through us."

She shifted her shaking pointer at the TV.

"And now the news is saying that the beam is putting people into a sleep that's killing them," she said.

No one knew what to say for an agonizing minute.

Dad let out a long sigh. "You want me to check on him?"

"No, let me go."

Kimberly stood. Her whole body shook, tears welled and rolled down her cheeks. Mom stood and put her arm around her.

"I'll come with you, sweetie," Mom said.

Dad and I stood quietly in the living room and watched them go upstairs. They disappeared down the hallway. We waited.

After a few minutes that seemed like an eternity, we heard muffled sobbing from the Maris's bedroom. I looked at Dad to see his reaction. He sighed, looked down, glanced toward the family room, and then looked at me.

"If Phillip is gone," he said. "Then being inside does us no good. There's nowhere to hide."

"If it got Philip, how come it didn't get the rest of us?" I asked.

Dad thought about that. All he could do was shrug and shake his head.

"Maybe the effects are different for everyone. We might not be out of the woods yet," he said. "Everyone's DNA is different. If we're dealing with geniuses from another world, who knows how advanced they are?

Hell, it's possible they could have a beam engineered for every individual genetic profile on Earth."

That was not a pleasant thought. I had nothing to say.

"I would doubt it goes that far," he said. "But it's affecting people differently. That much we do know. Maybe they're adjusting the waves as they go. We all may have different degrees of resistance to it. Who knows?"

I had a horrible thought.

"What if they're keeping certain people alive for some reason?"

"You do have a dark imagination, Son," Dad said. "Can't deny that possibility, though."

"What do you think we should do now?" I asked.

"I think we need to prepare ourselves for any possibility," he said. "By that, I mean we need to have a plan in place depending on how many of us survive. What if your mom is the last one? What if it's your younger sister?"

His own words anguished him.

"What would Madison do if she's the last one?" I asked.

I imagined my 12-year-old sister, the only survivor in this house, facing down the sort of men who attacked us in the truck. I couldn't bear it, but we'd have to plan for that possibility.

"Wow," I said.

It was the only reaction I could put into words.

"I know, Son," he said. "It's unpleasant to think about, but should these beams take me and leave you? Here's one of the things I need you to know—if something needs to be done, a man must do it. You understand? No matter how horrible or sick to your stomach it makes you or how much it makes you cry, you do it."

His confidence and determination gave me a sense of peace. I first started thinking beyond the flesh and blood life I had been living. He didn't come out and say it, but I sensed that Dad had learned, for all he'd been through, that it was better to die doing what was right than to live knowing you had failed to rise to the moment.

"You okay,?" Dad asked.

"We should show the kids how to access the emergency supplies," I said. "We should also make sure each of them can use a gun."

He was pleased I pivoted to new thinking so quickly.

"Yes, you're right," he said. "We should start that right away, right now. Kimberly's kids are going to need to be kept distracted for now.

"Tell you what, I'll start them on that right now. We don't know when the next attack will come and who it might take. You stay here and see if your mom and Kimberly need help."

Dad went into the family room. I heard him stop the movie and tell them he had some fun new activities for them to do, that he needed them to be his helpers and had important jobs for them. He made it sound like a children's morning show. It brought back fond memories of how he made me so excited to mow the lawn or paint the garage or some other horrible chore I should've hated but did because he convinced me it would be fun.

He marched them out of the family room and down to the basement, where the lesson would begin.

Now alone, I paced back and forth in the living room, trying to think of how I could be helpful, but instead obsessing over how slow time crawled.

Mom and Kimberly came slowly down the stairs. I froze. Kimberly's face was red, tear-streaked, a mask of shock.

"Where are the kids?" she whispered.

I pointed down toward the basement. "They're with Dad."

She nodded.

"Let's get Kimberly something to drink," Mom said.

I went into the kitchen and got her a glass of ice water. When I came back, they were sitting on the sofa. Kimberly had tissues in each hand as she dried her eyes. She was trying to keep herself under control, knowing the kids could come rushing back into the room at any minute.

"I can't believe this is happening," Kimberly said. "It just doesn't seem real."

Mom sat next to her and rubbed her back. I watched the anguish on Mom's face. I knew she thought of her own family. What if one of us were next?

I handed her the water, and she thanked me. She took a long drink.

"Water never tasted so good," she said.

She looked up at me. The pain in her eyes broke my heart.

"I hate to ask you this," she said. "But would you mind going up and checking on Philip yourself? I need another opinion."

I glanced at Mom, who shook her head in agreement.

I trotted up the stairs and down the hall, wanting to finish it quickly. In their bedroom, I found Philip on his side facing the door. His eyes were closed, and his arms were folded before him. It looked to all the world like he was enjoying a peaceful evening nap.

I felt his pulse on his wrist and his left ear. Nothing. I watched his chest for any rise and fall. I held my fingers under his nostrils, also nothing. His skin was undeniably cool. After that, I shook him real hard. I tugged on his hair, twisted his nipple, and squeezed his hamstring. I tried just about every locker room prank I could think of. He didn't budge. For the first time, I looked at a dead body.

There was nothing else to do. I returned downstairs and gave them a look of grim confirmation as I thought my dad might've done it.

"Maybe we should go outside to get some air," I said. "Dad says it doesn't matter if we're inside or not now that . . ."

"Yes, come on, Kim," Mom said. "Let's get you some air. There's sunshine left."

She helped Kimberly to her feet. I led them out the patio door and onto the deck. Kimberly took a deep breath, trying any way she could to reset her emotions and try to adjust to the new contours of her life.

"I don't know what to say to the kids," she said. "And the kids, my God, what if they're next?"

She started to break down again, but Mom quickly rubbed her back and massaged her shoulders.

"Now you listen," Mom said. "We'll be here for you. And this may start hitting all of us, so we'll have to be as strong as we can for each other. Okay?"

She nodded and dropped down onto a lounger. She stared into the clouds in the approaching night, not seeing them. She had been so full of life and smiles just twenty-four hours ago. Now, she looked like she hadn't slept in years, with no hope of doing so in the near future.

The ships continued to crisscross overhead, silent, menacing, and relentless. There were no more attacks as the night came in total. An awful, heavy sickness fouled the air. Philip was dead, and the rest of us waited for our turn. Any potential outcome was horrible. It wasn't easy to find hope.

Dad had the kids outside. After a very strict lecture about safety and the proper operating and handling of a weapon, he let them fire the revolvers. He explained how to handle intruders, taught them some basic first aid, showed them how to make their food stores last, how to keep track of news and information and figure out who to trust and how to act.

I thought it was an awful lot to cram into their little skulls, but they repeated everything to him perfectly whenever he went back and quizzed them on what they learned. They were really into it.

Mom and Dad prepared a late-night snack. Mom decreed that we ought to carry on as best we could. We needed food and rest and would continue to have them as long as possible.

Dad and Mom went with us to the beach while Kimberly took Sebastian and Lydia upstairs to their room. She had told them their dad was feeling sick and needed to rest. It wasn't as if he had died of a heart attack or cancer. The circumstances were just bizarre. She wasn't yet sure how to break the news to them or to explain it. So, in the meantime, as far as they were concerned, their father was sleeping off a twenty-four-hour bug.

They sensed this wasn't the truth but wanted to believe it enough to accept it.

I came out of my room, having changed clothes. I rushed past their door but couldn't help but overhear.

Kimberly whispered to them. "Your dad's not feeling well. He needs extra rest. But go ahead and tell him goodnight, okay?"

It took enormous effort for her to keep her composure and act like all was ordinary as she allowed her children to say goodbye to their father. It was the greatest act of emotional courage I had ever witnessed. It fortified me for what might come for my family.

Snack time was far more pleasant than I had anticipated. The kids were lively, joking, and carrying on, probably further than they would typically be allowed, but we desperately needed their positive energy.

We settled in the family room afterward. We watched a family movie that didn't satisfy anyone, but it was a pleasant enough way to pass the time and keep everyone diverted.

It was almost dark. The movie was over. Three young girls slept on the couch in a pile of arms, legs, and pajama cotton. Sebastian asked his mother if he could read his comic books until he fell asleep. She smiled and nodded, and he was gone. Mom stood and stretched and said she wanted to take a bath, and if anyone had to get in there first, they had better do so now. It was one o'clock in the morning.

No one else had to go, so Mom left the room. She passed my chair as she left. She glanced down, and when our eyes met, she reached out and grabbed my hand and squeezed it, then kissed the top of my head.

Dad, Kimberly, and I sat together in silence. Kimberly looked at the two of us and gave us a tired smile.

"Just so you know, you don't need to worry about me," she said. "Till death do us part, I suppose. It was going to end sometime, I guess. I didn't think it would be so soon, so . . . weird. Just don't feel like you have to make any small talk. It hurts a lot, but I think it's good that it does. I just need time."

We accepted the terms of her silence.

Dad was soon into a novel. I did some push-ups. A sense of calm had just settled in when the beam came again. The three of us stood up to wait and see what happened.

"Maybe we ought to be sitting down," Dad said. "Just in case."

We all sat down.

It was the same sensation as before. The beam shook through the house in a steady, lazy sweep. It tickled our guts and messed up our hair and was gone. It came and went, and the three of us watched each other, waiting for sleep to suddenly take us. We were still awake.

Kimberly immediately looked at the girls on the couch. They had already been asleep when the beam came. Dad and I thought of it, too. We rushed to the couch and gently shook the children.

Only Lydia opened her eyes. Sophia and Madison, my two perfect and beautiful little sisters, remained asleep.

REALITY

D ad knew the girls had fallen asleep forever. He dropped into his chair with a look of shock. Never had he looked ready to give it all up. His eyes were wide and wet with grief.

Kimberly made sure Lydia was comfortable, then ran upstairs to check on Sebastian.

Sophia and Madison looked so peaceful, their faces smooth, beautiful, and perfect. There was no way some sleazy alien beam could kill them so easily. I had promised to watch over them. Now, all I could do was stand there? The stress of the never-ending nightmare gripped my body. My breathing quickened, and my chest grew tight. If I ever got my hands on one of those creatures from another world, I vowed to twist its head clean off.

I gently shook the girls, refusing to give up for several minutes. I continued until Dad put a gentle hand on my shoulder. Tears spilled over my cheeks despite my efforts to hold them in. When I looked at Dad, his eyes were focused upstairs, where Mom had gone to take a bath. He left to check on her. I had a horrible feeling as I watched him ascend the stairs. He looked old for the first time.

While he was gone, Kimberly came down with Sebastian, who was groggy and cranky but awake. She had him curl up on the loveseat. Lydia crawled onto her mother's lap, looking around and curious about what was happening. She stayed quiet until she drifted off again. Kimberly looked alarmed momentarily but realized her children had been unaffected this time. So, she hugged her tight and let her sleep.

The only thing I could think of was to take a blanket and place it over them. I turned to look at Kimberly, who watched me. Her eyes were tired and hollow. She mouthed, "I'm so sorry." I know she would have hugged me if not for Lydia asleep on her lap.

Dad came slowly down the stairs, looking like it took all his strength to stay upright. His shirt and pants were soaked. He paused at the bottom step and looked at me. He didn't need to speak the words. Mom was gone. He'd had to lift her out of the tub.

I was hardly the first person to deal with so much shock and pain all at once. I was only the latest to walk down that well-trodden path with inner shredding wounds so severe you wonder how you continue to breathe. It is a living nightmare that not only can't be comprehended, it shows no sign of ending anytime soon.

We all had the same look of stoic exhaustion. Only so far can you ratchet up human anguish before the heart and mind resign themselves to living in a new world of pain.

By the following day, there had been two attacks. They had killed four of us, and five remained. Kimberly did her best to console us, but it was everything she could do to keep her own sanity under control. We shared the grief now, and everyone understood where everyone was coming from.

"So, what do we do now?" Kimberly asked.

At first, I was surprised. I had a mindset preparing me to die. The idea that life could, indeed, should, go on had not occurred to me, and I don't know if it would have if Kimberly hadn't spoken up.

"The thing to do is continue with life," Dad said. "There's a good chance this is the end for the rest of us, too. Our only option is to accept it and keep moving forward."

He looked at me for my reaction. I looked at my sisters together on the couch, under the blanket I used to cover them. Before, they had seemed peacefully asleep. But now they were clearly dead.

"Kimberly and I have a few years on you, Colby," Dad said. "It's only a little bit easier for us to accept what might be at an end, considering how we've had some life—marriage and children and whatnot. But this is being forced upon us. I can't tell you how to react, but you'll feel better about yourself if you accept it. Be defiant."

It was true that I had some fun times, and now I faced the end of not having lived a life I had chosen and built for myself. But as I stared at my sisters, I realized how few choices we have in life. I couldn't choose to keep my family alive. I couldn't choose to keep myself alive. But how I faced my death, should it come, well, that was something I could choose.

"I say we give everyone a proper burial," I said. "I think burying everyone at sea would be nice. We can take them out on the boat and let them go. After that, we tend to things — keep the property fortified, hunt, fish for food, and let's act as if we know this is all gonna work out and that we'll make it."

I watched them to see what they thought. Dad had a smile on his face. Kimberly had a look of grateful hope, glad I had set it.

"You know, the man says we're supposed to take them to these medical centers," Dad said.

He asked it as if it were a challenge.

"To hell with that," I said. "I won't let Mom and the girls be dumped into some fire pit, and you know that's what they're doing."

"I agree, Son," Dad said. "No way I'd allow that either."

He looked at Kimberly.

"No way," she said.

Dad took a deep breath. "Okay, then. We'll let our loved ones rest where they are for tonight. Tomorrow, we'll get some lumber from the garage, make a few coffins, take them out on the boat, and put them in the sea, back to God."

It was nice to have some decisions made. For now, we were all numb. And as we learned, as time went on, that was the best time to try to get some rest. The pain would ebb and flow like the tide, rending our minds and emotions to the brink of destruction, and then we'd be numb again.

Knowing that any moment could be our last was a weird feeling. Even though I had witnessed this very thing, it was still challenging to get my mind around the fact that death was around every corner, under every piece of furniture, hiding in the air we breathed. The craft continued overhead. They had a slight glow in the night.

We decided to sleep in the same room so we could check on one another. I can't tell you how I fell asleep that night, but we had prepared each other as best we could. From now on, there were hugs and kisses before bed, statements of love. Dad led us in prayers to help us trust and be courageous and look forward to a reunion in Heaven when it was all over. I said my prayers privately, trying to get myself right with God, confessed my sins, and resolved to meet this and any new challenge with faith and courage.

That first horrible night, I was reminded of that old children's prayer my mom used to lead me in every night before bed:

Now I lay me down to sleep, I pray the Lord my soul to keep, if I should die before I wake, I pray the Lord my soul to take.

Never had I said a prayer so earnestly.

I woke with a start the next morning. Everyone else was up. Kimberly prepared breakfast in the kitchen. I caught the aroma of cooking bacon and instantly felt a little better. Sebastian and Lydia watched TV. I staggered into the kitchen, bleary-eyed, trying to shake off the morning fog. Kimberly saw me and smiled, although her eyes were still dead, and her hands shook.

"Good morning!" she said.

That was when I first fell in love with her without realizing it. Her incredible heart and bravery amazed me, the selflessness it took to give me a cheery greeting.

"Want some coffee?" She asked.

"Yeah, thanks," I said.

She poured me a cup and set it on the table. I sat down and placed the coffee under my face so the coffee-infused steam could enter my lungs and work its magic to wake me up. There was a noise outside, and I looked around, puzzled.

"Your dad's out in the garage," she said. "He's been working on some coffins."

It seemed strange that 'coffins' was now a casual part of our vocabulary. I stood to help Dad.

"Sit down, Hon," she said. "Have some breakfast. We need to keep eating."

She set a plate before me covered in scrambled eggs, bacon, and toast. I don't remember ever being so hungry, so satisfied by a meal.

She joined me at the table with her coffee. She seemed satisfied that I had such a hearty appetite. I mostly kept my head down as I ate. It felt awkward, just the two of us sitting there in silence. I glanced up occasionally and caught her looking at me. She would quickly smile and look away. In those moments when she sipped her coffee and looked out the window, I would take my turn to look at her.

I'd seen her in the morning, before she dressed and showered, many times throughout several family vacations together. That morning, I saw her differently for the first time. I noticed she was infinitely more beautiful than my adolescent teenage brain had ever comprehended, even with her sleep-matted hair, threadbare pajamas, and haggard, makeup-free face.

She gave me a quick, shy glance and got up. She poured out the remnants of her coffee and rinsed her mug.

"I'm going to go clean up and get ready for the funeral," she said, drying her hands.

Kimberly felt the best mental course was to face things head-on and not deny what was happening. She glanced toward the family room where her children watched TV.

"After that, I'm going to have to tell them about their dad," she said. "No idea how I'm going to do that."

"You've done an excellent job facing up to things as they are," I said. "I think you should do the same with them. Sometimes, you're not old enough to hear something until you hear it."

She nodded in agreement. "Wise words."

She paused on her way out of the room and ran her fingers through my hair.

"And you're going to have to do something about this catastrophic bedhead, sir," she said.

She squeezed my shoulder as she went upstairs.

After breakfast, I dressed and freshened up. On the deck, I scanned the sky. The ships continued overhead, like drones following the same mind. It became a common sight. Even though the beams only came occasionally, the UFOs were ever-present. I waited for the sound or feel of that approaching pulsation, but it was a peaceful morning for the moment.

Dad had finished cutting the wood when I found him in the garage. He had one coffin done and was working on a wider-than-average box I assumed was for my mom and sisters to share. He sensed my presence.

"Morning, Son," he said. "Beautiful day."

Having something for his hands to do focused his mind away from his grief.

"There was another beam this morning, around seven," he said. "Did you feel it?"

"No."

"It was the third one."

I must have been zonked not to have felt it.

"Didn't affect any of us this time," he said. "It has to be tied to our physiology somehow."

"These aliens are scientists, for sure."

"So far, the beams are coming every six hours, give or take."

"That gives us some warning, at least," I said.

"You know, part of what chaps my ass about this whole thing is the unlikelihood that we'll ever get justice," he said. "Probably a waste of mental energy. Still, it would be nice to get my hands around the throat of one of those bloody bastards."

I almost laughed. I'd had the same thought. Imagine if we both caught one of them?

There was a stack of cut boards leaning against a table saw. He saw me looking at the boards and saw puzzlement in my face.

"I'm making boxes for all of us," he said. "You just never know, Son. This way, we have something ready for everyone."

He talked me through the process of making a coffin. It was mid-morning when we finished the last coffin. Dad went to the small refrigerator in the corner and grabbed a beer for each of us. We drink silently in the heat, satisfied and grateful for the distraction.

We went to the deck and found Kimberly and her kids crying together. She had told them about Philip. Dad and I snuck past them quietly into the house.

"It's time to take care of our ladies," he said.

I wrapped Madison and Sophia in the favorite blankets they brought with them. Upstairs, I found Dad buttoning up the dress he put on Mom. He saw me come in. He looked at his wife to ensure she was ready, then turned and left to give me a few moments. I had to will myself to breathe.

"Bring her down when you're ready, will you?" he said.

"Dad?"

He paused at the door.

"How much pain can a human being endure?" I asked.

"In my experience? Always a little more," he said.

He left me alone. I sat on the bed and took her hand. It was cold. That made me very uncomfortable, but I held on anyway. I thanked her for everything she had done for me. I told her I loved her. Nothing poetic or eloquent, but the words were honest.

I rolled back time, strolling through my memories and bringing up a few favorite times, thinking that maybe, wherever she was in heaven, she might be seeing the same thing — Christmases, better vacations, birthdays, a few times she had to smack a bully before I was big enough to do it myself. By the time I had revisited those memories, I was smiling.

I had never picked my mother up before, and despite our size difference, I was surprised at how light she was.

I carried her out to the deck. Dad had the coffins lined up. Philip lay peacefully in his, covered in a blanket. Kimberly and the kids were crying. Madison and Sophia were in the larger box. I ran my hands through their hair and told them goodbye. I thought my heart would stop.

Dad adjusted the girls as I laid Mom down in the coffin. We nailed the lid shut, and that was, without a doubt, the most challenging part of the entire process.

Everything was ready, and I helped Dad carry the boxes to the pier and lower them into our small boat. Sebastian helped us carry his dad's coffin.

He remained stoic from then on. He also kept a discrete eye on his watch. The next beam was due soon.

On the pier, Dad said a benediction for the dead. He asked if anyone else wanted to speak. We all remained silent. There wasn't enough room on the boat for everyone to ride out. Dad suggested that he take them out alone. No one argued.

Kimberly stood with their children before her, watching Dad speed away. She looked so alone in that moment I couldn't bear it. I came up behind her and put my hands on her shoulders. She lowered her head to rest her cheek against my hand. We had no idea how much longer any of us would live.

Dad didn't go far. He stopped and gently let the coffins slip into the sea.

The indifferent cruelty of circumstance was nothing if not predictable. We returned to the deck after the draining experience of the funeral. We relaxed, listened to the waves, and watched the sun work its way to the horizon. I wondered if those of us still sitting there would be the new family unit surviving this ordeal. We managed to force down a meager lunch. Everyone was quiet.

Dad stretched out on the lounger, his arms folded, looking at the horizon. He expected the next beam soon, if his time estimates were accurate. He asked me not to say anything to Kimberly. He worried it would only add to her stress, and it was possible he might be wrong.

She occupied another lounger with the children lying on either side of her under her arms. I sat upright in my lounger. It was a weird feeling not to know if I could rest, what I should think about, and whether it was okay to start processing anything that happened so far. Coming to grips with it all was dangerous. It could all come undone again in new ways. And that's precisely what happened.

Around one o'clock, the attacking ship came from the north. It shook the trees hard, and the sand danced on the deck. As the humming vibration came closer and it was seconds away, Dad looked over at me and smiled. It was the most peaceful I've ever seen him. He winked and nodded at me as if to say everything between us was settled and okay. He turned away, closed his eyes, and laid back, ready for whatever was coming.

I glanced at Kimberly. She, too, had her head leaned back with her eyes closed. She held her children tight. They clutched her clothing. It seemed like a brave way to face things, so I closed my eyes, too.

The beam swept across the property as it had two times before. There was still a jolt of terror as the mechanisms and motives of the beam remained a mystery.

I opened my eyes after the sensation had passed. The ships still droned overhead. They ruined an otherwise perfectly blue sky. I knew at some point, I would have to look to my left and right and see what, if anything, had happened. I had survived a third time. How many more times would there be?

I heard sniffling and looked to my left. Kimberly cried out whatever tears she had left. Sebastian and Lydia were gone, eyes closed and still in her arms. Kimberly looked out to the waves, mouthing words to herself silently, her face wet with tears. She ran her fingers through her children's hair. I had to look away.

Dad lay in his lounger to my right, completely relaxed and dead. It seemed so anti-climatic for someone who had lived such a life of adventure and accomplishment to fade away on his deck lounger. I watched him for a few minutes, expecting him to rise up, having overcome it somehow. He would snap to his feet and tell me how he had outsmarted it. He would draw up the plan of victory, and we would carry it out together and show the world how to do it.

But there was no awakening. There was only reality.

Leo Swanson. Army Second Lieutenant. Millionaire. Husband. Father. Lord of the Manor. He who could fix anything, build anything, and bring wisdom to anything, was dead.

SURVIVIORS

Like zombies, we were. For an hour, we sat just as we were when it happened. I stared up at the ships passing overhead. They looked lazy and indifferent. I had to keep my eyes off Kimberly. She was so distraught I worried her heart would stop. I couldn't blame her. She stroked her children's hair, waiting for them to wake up. I had to look away.

What kind of beings were these aliens? Why were they doing this? Were they like humans in that some of them opposed this attack? Did they have statesmen among them to argue for our right to live? I thought of anthills I had detonated with firecrackers as a boy. Maybe that's how they saw us.

I looked over at Dad. He could have been napping on a Sunday afternoon. I couldn't stand it, having him lay there. He would have hated it, too.

It took all my strength and reserve to get him into the coffin he'd built for himself. Kimberly saw me struggle.

"You want some help?" she asked in a small voice.

I told her I could do it. She looked away to give me some privacy. He looked handsome and dignified lying there. I picked up the lid and felt a surge of emotion.

"I'll remember what you told me," I said to him.

I nailed the lid shut, tapping the nails as gently as possible. I thought Kimberly needed some privacy, so I went inside.

"Can you stay?" she asked. "I don't want to be alone."

"Sure."

I returned to my seat.

"It's a parent's worst nightmare, you know? For their children to die," she said. "But this is worse than a nightmare. I couldn't have imagined this."

I was suffering plenty, but I knew her pain had reached depths I couldn't imagine.

"I don't want to let them go. But, if I stay here with them, I will die. I think I should live, to honor their memory, right? But I want to die. I hope I go to sleep, too."

She looked at me with a look so seared with anguish I didn't recognize her.

"Tell me what to do, Colby."

No way had I lived long enough to know what to tell her, but I had to think of an honest answer. I glanced at Dad's coffin.

"Dad would've told me to accept what I can't change," I said. "Maybe the first step to getting better is acceptance."

"Well, I can't accept it, but I see your point. I'll have to try to live with it. That much I think I can do. I'll try. Good enough?"

"I will if you will."

She smiled. "I know. You're hurting, too. Sorry."

We sat on the deck for another three hours. Conversation came and went. She would weep for a while, then calm down and rest. She never said what the trigger was, but out of nowhere, she took a deep breath.

"Okay, I'm ready," she said.

I gestured toward the empty coffins. "Do you want me to help you . . ."

"Yes, please."

"You want to change their clothes or anything?"

"No. No special preparations or anything," she said. "This is what they were wearing when they were taken from me, and this is how I want to see them for the last time."

I carefully put them in the coffin side-by-side. They didn't look dead, just asleep. There was no getting used to it. When that was done, I made an excuse and went inside to give her time alone. I stood in the kitchen and drank glass after glass of water, not knowing what might come next. I watched her from the window. She talked to them, stroked their hair, and sat silently for a few minutes.

Eventually, she sat up and looked around, wondering where I was. I took the cue and went outside.

"I'm ready," she said, looking like a small weight had been lifted. "Let's go ahead and do it."

For the second time that day, we had a group funeral. We re-created the formalities of just a few hours before. We got the coffins loaded on the boat and motored out to sea. They bobbled on the water's surface as we slid them in as gently as possible. It took a few minutes for them to sink. We put our arms around each other as the last corners of wood slipped beneath the waves.

Watching those humble pine boxes disappear to the bottom of the ocean was the hardest part of it all. Oh, how we cried. It was the hardest I had ever wept in my life. And it must've taken everything out of me because I haven't cried since. Just spent, I guess.

We returned to shore, tied the boat, and trudged back to the house. In the silence we shared on the deck, exhausted, I got a sense of how strange my world had become. Kimberly and I were of different generations. And while we knew each other from spending so much time with our families over the years, we weren't that close. The age gap was too vast for us to be friends, so we were already a mystery to each other.

And now, not only had we entered this bizarre new world as acquaintances, we were now different people. I had no idea what to expect, no idea if she would even continue living in the house or leave. I knew we had lots to discuss, but it was not the time.

"We should eat something," she said. "I know we need to start conserving food, but I could use a big dinner."

"Yeah, a big meal would hit the spot."

"And listen, I know there's a lot of things we need to talk about as far as how it's going to be moving forward," she said. "Do you mind if we wait a few days for that? Can we just be housemates? We can work together to maintain things. I don't know what the future holds, and I don't have the energy to process right now."

"Yeah, that works for me," I said.

What did she mean about the future? What future?

"But there is one thing I don't think will wait, though," I said.

She looked apprehensive.

"This beam," I said. "We should make arrangements in case one of us goes and the other is left. I don't mean to be insensitive."

"Don't you think it would have done us in by now?" she asked. "I'm starting to think you and I have some kind of immunity to this."

I was shocked. Immunity hadn't crossed my mind until then. My working assumption was that Kimberly and I would also end up dead. The only question was when and who would go first.

"Seriously, what if it's not gonna hurt us?" she asked. "That's what I mean about figuring out how things will go forward."

Part of her hoped for the eternal sleep. I wasn't sure how to react to that. It hadn't occurred to me that surviving was the least attractive of her options.

"Yes, you're right. I agree that planning can wait," I said. "But just in case, I'll arrange it so you don't have to try to carry me in case I fall asleep and you don't."

She snorted a quick laugh as she looked me up and down as if she hadn't noticed before that I was three times her size. If I went first, it would take all she had to get me out the door. She must've pictured it because she started giggling and eventually giggled herself into racking guffaws, which started me laughing.

"Okay, Colby," she said. "I'll leave it for you to figure something out."

She gave me a quick hug and went inside to prepare some food. I watched her leave, then checked my watch. The last beam had arrived at one o'clock, almost on the nose. Dad was right. The beams came on a six-hour schedule, which meant the next one was due at seven, only two hours away.

In my room, I checked my rifle and revolver. I tried to put myself in Dad's mind. I didn't have to wonder too hard what he would've done because I had witnessed what he had done. When Mom and the girls went to sleep, he immediately went to work. He did what he considered his duty: to do what had to be done.

Out front, I found the gate blocking the front drive was still smashed flat. Well, there was a job. I wouldn't have known what to do if it had been a week ago. But since I'd helped Dad put up the fence around the property, I replaced the poles, refitted the chain-link fence, and reset the razor wire with little trouble, aside from a few cuts.

After that, I checked the rest of the fence. Everything looked secure. There were no signs of humans or animals trying to get through. Next, I took a food inventory. Dad had stocked plenty of dry goods to sustain at least a family of four, if not more, for six months. Kimberly and I could stay here a year or more if it took that long to wait things out.

The doors, windows, and shutters were locked and strong. Dad had done such an excellent job of thinking ahead and preparing that there wasn't much left for me to do but maintain what he started. The only question mark was things like electricity and running water. The last news reports we had seen indicated the death toll, at least nationwide, was running into the millions with no signs of slowing down. How long could infrastructure be maintained?

Kimberly was busy in the kitchen, so I went into the family room and turned on the TV at low volume. There were no more talking heads. The emergency broadcast system was now the only thing on any channel. There were no more pretty faces reading their lines. Instead, it was a dull, monotonic voice reading words visible in white lettering against a stern, official-looking navy blue background with a FEMA logo in the upper left corner.

Officials assured us that those steering the ship at utilities and power companies had immunity from alien attack. Electricity, gas, and water would continue to flow.

Something didn't sit well about that. They knew certain people had immunity, but after watching for nearly thirty minutes, they did not hint at how the rest of us could know who had it, who didn't, and how we could get it. As usual, the authorities knew more than they were letting on.

Then came the announcement that anyone who had survived seven alien attack beams should immediately go to the nearest government shelter. Trucking was spotty at best, so supplies would soon run out, and shelters would soon be the only place for food. After that, a map appeared on the screen for our immediate area, with yellow dots indicating shelter locations. Presumably, people across the United States saw maps of their area.

Kimberly and I had survived four waves of attacks. Another one was due soon. How did authorities arrive at seven as the magic number? Of course, they weren't saying.

Information began to repeat. I shut off the TV. I was about to go into the kitchen and tell Kimberly what I had learned when I felt rumblings of another wave approaching. It was nearly seven. Time had gotten away from me.

"Colby?" Kimberly called from the kitchen.

We met in the living room, and I waved her outside.

"Come on!" I said.

We ran out onto the deck. I crawled into one of the open coffins. If this was to be my last moment, I didn't want Kimberly to have to exhaust herself dragging me to the beach.

"I'm sorry," she said. "But I'm not laying down in that thing."

"Don't worry about it," I said. "If it's your time, I won't have trouble moving you."

She knelt next to me and took my hand.

The beam came from the South. It ran along the deck, gave us that tickling, slightly nauseating feeling, and was soon gone. I took stock of how I felt. There was no fatigue or heaviness of the eyelids. I survived wave number five. I opened my eyes to see Kimberly looking down at me with a weary smile.

She looked disappointed that she had survived.

After I told Kimberly about the official limit of survival and Dad's estimate of the time cycle, we kept careful watch. We wanted to make sure we were together for the seventh time. If we both lived through that, it would be time to discuss our future.

We spent the rest of the evening keeping our minds and hands busy to avoid the clock and thus slow it down. We weeded the flowers around the deck and sides of the house, took what had to be the third or fourth inventory of the storage house, and fired some practice shots. After dark, we were too tired to do anything but watch a movie.

Beam six came at one a.m. She came into my room and shook me awake. We hurried out to the deck and waited.

We lived.

Back inside, we went and returned to sleep.

She woke me again at 6:45.

"Do you mind if we wait on the beach this time?" She asked. "I don't want to be laying in some box, and I'm tired of sitting on that deck when it goes over. If it's my time, I want to be on the beach, watching the sea."

"Sounds good to me," I said. "And I'm going to dress for it, just in case."

"That's a good idea," she said. "Meet you outside?"

I found her sitting on the beach with her feet buried in the sand. Her knees were drawn up, and she hugged her legs, staring at the incoming tide. She wore a black, one-piece bathing suit under an unbuttoned beach dress. The sun had been up for over an hour, and she looked like she'd been lit for a romantic movie. Next to her was a bottle of wine and two glasses.

"Not fancy, I know," she said. "But wearing this makes me think of being here with my family."

"You look very nice," I said.

She looked me over as I sat down next to her. I wore my football jersey and a pair of jeans.

"The jeans represent the blue-collar path I've chosen," I said. "The jersey symbolizes my history."

"Excellent choice," she said. "You wear it well."

She handed me the bottle of wine and a corkscrew.

"Here, open this," she said. "May as well have a toast, even though I'm contributing to the delinquency of a minor."

It galled me to be called a minor. I got the cork open and poured us each a glass. She raised hers. I joined her.

"Here's to facing the future with faith and courage," she said. "Come what may."

We clinked our glasses together.

"Here, here," I said.

We finished the wine just as the beam came from behind us from the east. She shimmied close to me until our bodies touched shoulder to foot. I put my arm around her, and she huddled into the crook of my arm and wrapped her arms around me. Her breathing was fast, and she squeezed me tight. I pulled her close, closed my eyes, and waited.

The wave passed through us and out to sea. We watched the water mist into the air as the wave swept over it. By then, we knew from bitter experience that the beam's effects would be known within thirty seconds.

Those thirty seconds came and went. We relaxed our grip but still held each other. Seven waves had passed through us. According to official sources, that meant we were immune. Survivors. We shared a wide-awake look.

"Still here!" she said.

STARTING OVER

The beam was no threat to us. The world had collapsed and became far more dangerous than usual. Our families were gone, wiped out entirely in less than a day. We didn't know what to do next other than go about our daily routines. Silence echoed everywhere after the passing of our loved ones. The ships continued to fly in indecipherable patterns overhead. The beams had ceased. The attack—this phase of it, anyway—was over. We no longer feared sleep, not for that reason. I slept in my tower room. Kimberly retired to the room she had shared with Philip. The only certainty—we knew we would wake up the next morning.

A week went by, then two. Numbers on a calendar faded in importance as days became periods of light and dark. We arranged food rations; the fresh food we'd brought for vacation was eaten first. I made a daily check of the house and grounds. Kimberly would join me sometimes. We'd play games, watch TV, go for walks. All very friendly and comfortable. We talked a lot, mostly about what had happened, why, and the future. Kimberly and I made decent housemates.

There were days I wouldn't see her at all. She would stay in her room and never come out. The first time that happened, I was compelled to knock on her door and make sure she was still alive. In a weepy voice from behind the door, she told me she was fine and needed some time alone. That happened two or three times a week.

I missed my family as well. Something about the finality of their deaths made things easier for me. I don't mean to sound odd or callous. They were gone. There were no more chats, no more laughter, no more nothing. It was as if the aliens had abducted them rather than killed them. There was no option but to continue unless I planned to spend the rest of my life doing nothing but thinking about how awful their passing had been. I know Kimberly had a different way of dealing with it, but the only way I could go forward was to place their memories on a shelf in a special room in my mind and continue living.

The cellular network was iffy out there in the boonies, to begin with. After things went to hell, connecting and getting word from family and friends was impossible. Kimberly was an only child. Her brother had died in a car accident in high school. Her parents had been dead for ten years. She was alone. My extended family did not survive the beams and the aftermath, although I wouldn't know that until years later.

The emergency broadcast system still urged people to go to the shelters. You had to go to the shelters if you wanted food, water, extra clothing, and medical care. Stores were looted, and shipping was erratic at best.

Everything was centered in the shelters. I was too young to be paranoid, but I had a bad feeling. Going where there was food, shelter, and protection made sense. The counter argument was that historically, governments herding people into camps didn't have a good reputation.

Shouldn't manufacturing and shipping have continued if they had found a way to identify the immune and get them into critical jobs? At least in a limited capacity? Kimberly thought it was because order had broken down entirely in the cities, and being there was no longer safe.

Life continues, no matter who owns the skies or how many trucks are on the road. This desire to continue living made me antsy as the days wore on. There was only so much to do in a day. It took little time to maintain the grounds and clean the house. When the chores to be done were finished, most of the day lay ahead. With my mind free to wander, I worried about what might come next.

Kimberly found me on the beach, pacing back and forth, watching the sea. The occasional ship went by in the distance, but nothing ever came close, no sign that they saw us or had any interest. We became negligent about keeping the back gate closed after being utterly alone for so long.

"You seem restless," she said.

"I am."

"Me, too," she said. "I thought maybe we'd be getting some answers by now. I keep waiting to hear that the Air Force shot these things out of the sky. It would be cool to see it happen."

"It would be cool if something happened," I said. "Makes me nervous. I thought the military would have settled this by now."

"I know what you mean. Feels like we're never returning to the old way of life."

"We have enough food for another year, probably," I said. "We could stay here, I suppose."

She swatted my arm. "Are you getting bored with me?"

"No, not at all!" I said, hoping I didn't sound too enthusiastic.

"Are you thinking we should go to the shelters?" she asked.

"No," I said. "I may sound like a tinfoil loony, but I don't trust the shelter business."

I didn't trust the shelter business, but there was more at play than that. Kimberly and I had a pleasant, peaceful coexistence here, but something seemed unfinished. We weren't friends, nor were we lovers. We shared a terrible grief and profound understanding, yet we couldn't discuss it. Damn right, I was restless.

Thoughts of her and I being a couple swirled in my head by then. For a long time, I dismissed it as a biological urge brought on by circumstance. She was the same age as my mother, and I was only 19, but she was a woman. I was a man. The idea that we should conform to the expectations of a world that no longer existed seemed bizarre to me. That's how it started. Not so much a feeling of lust or love toward Kimberly but a practical sense that she and I could build something together. I knew I could face this new world alone. Facing it with Kimberly and the ties we shared would be better. But facing it alone yet together? That didn't appeal to me. It was too soon to broach those subjects with her, so I decided to go through our routine for now.

"Yeah, I don't like the idea of going to the shelters either," she said. "I think we have a good thing here. You don't seem to mind hanging out with an old lady."

It was too obvious to tell her she wasn't an old lady, so I said nothing.

"You have to admit, though," she said. "I'm holding up well."

I turned to look at her. She glanced at me and shyly looked away. I watched her profile as she stared at the horizon. The wind tossed that beautiful mane of hair around. She sensed eyes upon her and turned to look at me again. She smiled, curious.

"I wouldn't want to do this alone," I said.

I ran my mouth after telling myself I didn't want to press ahead with my feelings. Her smile faded, and she pondered the intent of my words. She smiled and looked away and let the moment fade.

The Army showed up two days later. I was in the garage, going through lumber and wondering if there was anything I should be doing with it all. While in there, I heard someone hailing at the front gate. I walked out to find two soldiers in fatigues. They didn't see me right away. I considered ducking back into the garage. There were rumors of soldiers going rogue, warlords taking over territory, and looking for houses where they might find items, including women and children, to sell. Legit or not, there was no ignoring them. I decided it was better they knew the property was occupied and defended.

"Good afternoon, sir," said the first one.

"Good afternoon. What can I do for you, fellas?"

"We're checking houses up along this highway," he said. "Are you the only one here?"

The second soldier never said a thing. He watched me, appraising and forming opinions.

"Just me and my grandmother," I said. "We lost everyone else."

It seemed a safe answer in case their intentions were less than noble.

"She getting around okay?" he asked.

"Yeah, for her age, she gets along fine."

"You folks well-provisioned?" he asked.

"No, not really," I said.

It didn't seem wise to broadcast our large storage room.

"Then you folks should come with us. We have a bus out on the highway," he said. "Would be happy to give you a ride to the nearest shelter. Your grandmother can get medical care. They'll take good care of you until this is over."

"Has the Air Force started a counteroffensive?" I asked.

The soldiers exchanged a look.

"I'm sure they're planning something," he said. "We're not privy to that sort of information. We've been told that they don't know when this will be over, but they think it will be soon. How's that for specific?"

I had to admire his honesty.

"Well, I think I'm gonna stay here and wait it out a little longer," I said. "Lots of memories here. Hard to leave."

"Suit yourself," he said. "For now, all we can do is ask."

For now?

"The thing is, if I'm going to die, I want to do it here, in my own house," I said. "I don't want that beam knocking me to sleep forever in some bunk bed in a shelter," I said.

"I understand," he said. "But you know you're not gonna die from the beam. It's good to be an A-positive, right?"

I didn't follow what he was saying at first. "I was never better than a B student, I'm afraid."

"No, when I say A-positive, I'm talking about blood, not grades."

I still didn't get it.

"You have A-positive blood, sir," he said. "So do we. So does anyone who survived it. The beam was calibrated to take out all blood types but ours. That much we know. That much I can tell you."

I was shocked. Dad had guessed such a thing in theory. "That makes sense, I guess. Do you know why?"

"Way above my pay grade, pal," he said. "Tell you what, I'll mark this house as empty. You have a working vehicle?"

"I do."

"Well then, if things really start to go to hell, you should get to a shelter. They are well-defended, believe me."

That's partly what I was afraid of.

After they were gone, I checked the fence around the property. I also removed my weapons from the bedroom, determined not to be caught unarmed again. At dinner, I told Kimberly about the encounter. She, too, was taken aback by the fact that they were only asking "for now."

"What's your blood type?" I asked. "Do you know?"

"A-positive. Why?"

"Because that's the secret," I said. "The beams targeted people with certain blood types. I couldn't have told you before what my blood type was, but I'm sure I know now. Who knows why."

"Kinda creepy to think these aliens spared us," she said. "Why would they do that?"

The conversation died off as we ate. This happened often. We'd be chatting, and suddenly, we would both stop talking.

"You know," she said. "I always thought I'd live to be an old lady. When you think about that, it's in the context of the world you're living in. But the world as it is now? What it may become? I have no idea. I have no idea what comes next or what I will make of it. It just makes me . . . feel alone, tired."

"Plenty of handsome soldiers are out there if you decide to start again."

I regretted the line as soon as I had set it. Stupid and immature. She shot me a look, and I waited for the tears and anger directed at me. Instead, she was reflective, as if she had a thought that surprised her. She didn't share it with me, though.

"Huh. Interesting," was all she said.

She stretched out with her eyes closed to the sun and wind. I glanced for two seconds at her long legs and, of course, got caught. She grinned at me but didn't look offended.

"You can look at my legs if you want," I said.

She laughed—a nervous laugh or a dismissive one. I don't know.

"You wear that swimsuit all the time," I said. "Is there a reason? You never go swimming."

"It's the most comfortable I have, besides my birthday suit," she said. "Besides, we shouldn't let laundry pile up. Water and power might go out at any time, you know."

"I have noticed the water pressure is getting weak."

We were in the beginning of August by then. It was hotter than average. Simple clothing, quickly washed in the sink, made sense—one less thing to occupy our minds. My chosen wardrobe was even more straightforward —my gym shorts. I stayed cool and got a nice tan.

I know what you might be thinking: dressing down was not a case of practical decision-making but more of a man and a woman urging each other down the natural path humans follow when they're stuck alone. Remember that Kimberly was still too grief-stricken to see herself as a woman to be desired, and she still saw me as Leo and Robyn's kid.

In light of that, it was funny how that evening's mini-adventure began. I slept on my back, on top of the covers. I had just dozed off when I felt her hand on my shoulder. At first, I thought it was a dream. She pushed on my shoulder, up and down over and over, shaking me, trying to wake me up. My eyes fluttered open. I looked over to see her standing by my bed. In my drowsy state, I'm lucky I didn't yank her down onto the bed with me. I kept my wits about me.

"Something's going on outside," she whispered.

I flew out of bed. We took our rifles and went out the back of the house, onto the deck, and listened. A rumble sounded in the distance.

"A truck?" she asked.

"Sounds like it," I said. "Sounds far away, though. Like it's coming from the other side of the hill."

"Look!"

Also behind Blackjack Hill were shafts of iridescent light stabbing and undulating through the trees as if the light source was lowering into the trees. We walked further into the backyard and tried to get a better look.

"No way to tell what it is without hiking over the hill," I said.

"Hell with that," she said. "You think it's one of those ships?"

"Logical assumption."

"Are we in danger?"

"Possibly," I said. "I don't mean to sound forward, but we should sleep together."

Her eyes went wide in the moonlight.

"I worded that wrong. Sleep in the same room, I mean. For mutual protection."

"Got it. Yes, I agree."

After only a few minutes, the lights and the sounds were gone.

"If those things are starting to land . . ." she said.

"Could be those soldiers checking the forest for more people," I said. "Remember we heard an engine. A loud one. Probably diesel."

The woods were dense and uninhabited. There are few places for a craft to land. No real reason or roads for trucks to get up there. It could be camps of refugees had sprouted up there—all the more reason to keep an eye on the fence.

We stood together for ten more minutes, waiting for any indication that someone or something was coming toward us. All was still.

"I guess that's it," I said.

"I guess so."

"If you want to go in, I think it's okay," I said. "But I'd like to keep watch for a few more minutes."

"Okay. Maybe we could sleep in your sisters' room?" she asked. "Two beds?"

"Good idea."

"We can arrange something permanent tomorrow."

"I'll be inside in a few."

I watched the trees for another fifteen minutes. Not because I was afraid of what might be out there—that anxiety had died down—but because I feared joining Kimberly in a bedroom in the exhilarating coolness of a strange night.

The lights were out when I entered the bedroom, and she slept on the innermost bed. She'd left me the bed by the door, which I would've wanted. She lay on her side with her back to me, on top of the blankets, and lightly snored.

I studied her sleeping figure and admired her beauty. Her hair fanned out as if servants had spent hours brushing it. Her hips rose and fell in a perfect arch. Moonlight glistened off her toned legs. Delicate feet hung over the edge of the bed. Only then did I have a quiet moment to consider how beautiful she was. She looked so small and delicate and perfect. I felt a strong urge to protect that beauty at all costs. I couldn't say if I was in love yet. At my age, I couldn't have known for sure.

CAPTAIN SOLOMON

My growing feelings for Kimberly were always uppermost in my mind and became the center of my motivation to go on. I exercised self-control that was hard to imagine one year ago. The specter of death and the loss of our families still hovered over us. Kimberly would walk out to the beach and look over the waves, speaking to her husband and children. I knew there was no room in her heart for anyone else.

One evening at dusk, I joined her as she took an evening walk along the waves. My appearance startled her initially, but she just smiled and walked on. The setting sun cast a golden light so perfectly it seemed like God had created a tableau, especially for telling a girl how you felt.

We reached the end of the beach where the southern timberline began, then turned around and made our way back. I was on her right side, the sea to her left. I watched her as she watched the horizon. I sensed that she felt my gaze upon her cheek. She slowly turned to look at me. She didn't smile or look shy. She held my look as if she welcomed it.

I took that as encouragement, so I slowly reached for her hand. My fingers had crossed her palm. I was about to close my grip when she smoothly pulled her hand away and ran it through her hair. It was a blow, to be sure, but I didn't react. I just kept walking as if our hands had pressed together by accident.

We walked in silence, although I did notice she made a sly effort to fix her hair and adjust the top of her swimsuit. Was that for me? It seemed like a good sign.

I was embarrassed, so I kept to myself for a while. We didn't speak of it. Life continued, the two of us housemates, the future formless and never arriving.

It had been one month since we'd survived the seventh beam. That was when Captain Solomon showed up at our back gate around mid-morning. I spotted him from the kitchen window, standing there. He wasn't a large man. He was thin but in a way that suggested a surprising, wiry strength. His hair was black, and curly, and matched his dark eyes. His entire aura was dark. He was as old as my dad, I would've guessed. Something about how he stood there, expectant, as if he knew he would get what he had come for, made me nervous.

I pointed him out to Kimberly. She joined me at the kitchen sink and looked at him.

"Looks creepy," she said. "A refugee, you think?"

Refugees were something we expected to encounter a lot sooner than that day. Other than the raiders in the truck and the army men, no one had come by the property looking for shelter or food. That wasn't a surprise, considering how remote we were. It was possible, though, so we had taken some provisions and created care packages tied up in grocery bags. We would share them if needed. So far, no one had come.

Under no circumstances were we letting anybody onto the property or into the house unless I could physically subdue them on my own.

Kimberly went down for a care package as I shouldered my rifle. She gave me the sack as I walked out the patio door onto the deck.

"Watch close," I said. "If anything happens to me, and he makes his way in, shoot him dead. Don't hesitate."

We had discussed and even rehearsed such a scenario. Kimberly had practiced with the AR-15. We had never imagined such situations possible, but it was a new world with evolving rules.

The revolver was in the back of my shorts. I wasn't wearing a shirt, and anyway, it was best his first impression of me was how huge and fit I was.

It had the desired effect. I saw him looking me up and down as I approached. He kept a smile on his face. He tried to look friendly, but I saw fast thinking behind his eyes, the formation of dangerous plans.

He held his hands out at his side, fingers splayed. He smiled at me like I was an old friend.

"Whoa, take it easy there, friend," he said. "I'm just looking for some help, that's all."

That he was at the back gate meant that he had come from the sea—and there was a good-sized private boat in the distance—or he had hiked through the woods coming down from Blackjack Hill and whatever might be happening there.

"What can I do for you, mister?"

I stood back from the fence, out of his reach. My heart pounded like a piston, although I did an excellent job hiding my fear. The truth is, I acted as I thought Dad would have. He would've been reasonable and careful as long as possible and ruthless without mercy when he had no more choice.

The stranger pointed to the boat in the distance.

"My boat is over by the trees," he said. "Me and the wife and kids. We're running low on food and fuel. I could also use a place to stay for a while. What do you think? Could you folks help us out?"

Something about his use of the word "folks" raised a red flag.

"There's no 'folks' here," I said. "It's just me."

Something flickered in his eyes as if he knew he'd been caught knowing something he shouldn't. He looked up at the house on the property and nodded his head.

"Awfully big house for one man," he said.

"Here you go," I said.

I heaved the sack over the fence. It had canned goods, dry goods, and a jug of water. He watched it come over the fence but made no effort to catch it. It hit the sand and rolled a few inches. He glanced at it and looked at me again.

"I have no fuel. Sorry," I said.

He thought about what to do next.

"Does the army know you're here?" he asked.

"Maybe."

"So, no room at the inn, eh?" he asked.

"Afraid not," I said. "I've had some bad experiences. The care package is the best I can do."

He smiled in a way I did not like and glanced down at the sand for a moment. We both knew I wouldn't be seduced with fake, friendly small talk. When he looked back up, everything had changed.

"Well, I suppose we could do this all day," he said. "But I'd like to finish my business here before lunch."

I shifted the rifle and held it across my body. He didn't flinch. If it was possible, his eyes got even darker.

"Don't even bother with that, Sonny," he said through gritted teeth. "Two snipers are waiting to take your brains out when I give the signal."

There was no way to know if he was bluffing or telling the truth. My money was on the truth. He relaxed.

"Okay, let's calm down and be friends," he said. "They call me Solomon. Captain Solomon."

"That's not your real name?" I asked.

"New name for a new world."

"They call you that because of your wisdom?" I asked.

He grinned in a way I didn't like. "Because of the size of my harem."

A clearer picture of his intentions now appeared.

"Now, my offer is quite simple, but it is final and not open to negotiation," he said. "The woman you're living with in there? She comes with me. She'll be treated well, more or less, as long as she does what she's told when she's told."

My legs got wobbly.

"As for you, you'll have the privilege of joining my crew. This house will become my property. It'll form a nice base for me along the coast here. I'm expanding, you might say. Things are never going back to normal, Son, and you won't hold out here forever. And believe me, you don't want to go to the shelters."

"What's wrong with the shelters?" I asked.

"They're gathering people for these aliens, of course," he said. "You've seen different ships landing here and there, right?"

"I haven't," I lied. "Tell me something. How do you have an operation like this up and running so fast?"

"My friend, the signs of this happening have been in plain sight for anyone who didn't have their head in a dark place."

"What if I refuse your offer?" I asked.

"Then we'll take the property anyway. You've got it locked down pretty well, but we've gotten into tighter places than this. It's so much fun to see the surprise on a man's face when he . . . realizes what's coming.

After we take the house, we'll pass your lady around for a few days and let you watch. After we're done, I'll keep your heads as trophies. Think I'm kidding, chief? Is this my first rodeo?"

"I think you're telling the truth."

"Then what's it gonna be?" he asked.

When he asked the question, something caught his attention behind me. His eyebrows went up. He looked delighted. I knew what caught his eye, but I turned to look anyway.

Kimberly had strolled out onto the deck with a look of concern on her face. She held a rifle at her side. The look on her face asked me if everything was okay. I gave her a quick wink and turned back to face Solomon.

He looked like a hungry wolf.

"Oh, she is exquisite," he said. "Look at that body. Hard to contain myself."

"Why are you doing this?" I asked. "You could be helping people. How did you get here?"

The question didn't offend him.

"I thought I might be someone like you at first," he said. "I'd just keep to myself, wait things out, get a medal for being a good citizen. I had my own island just off Puget Sound—a wife and three daughters. Then the pirates came. I'll spare you the details.

"One night, I went aboard their boat. There were six of them. I should've been killed right away, but it turns out I'm very good at killing people.

"They didn't just take my family, Son. They took my sanity, and I was glad to be rid of it. My family was sacrificed for my sanity."

"I'm sorry about your family," I said. "But you didn't have to choose this path."

"Kill or be killed, my friend, kill or be killed," he said. "Anyway, that's enough time on Memory Lane. Give your answer right now."

"I'm choosing a different path from you, Solomon," I said. "Sorry, no sale."

He nodded, weary, as if I was a wayward son refusing to mow the lawn.

"Matters not to me either way, kid," he said.

He turned and walked away toward the timberline to the north. He left the care package in the sand. At the tree line, he and two riflemen I hadn't seen boarded a skiff hidden behind large chunks of driftwood. They motored away. Solomon faced me and waved. He shouted over the engine.

"I'm looking forward to meeting her!"

I thought about rushing through the gate onto the beach to open fire and kill them all. They were already too far away. There is no way to know how many more men hid in the trees.

I didn't expect him to return that night. Someone like him enjoyed cruelty. He would make us live with the possibility for at least a few weeks, maybe more. He had no reason to hurry. I had no way to strike at him first.

Kimberly could tell something ominous had happened. I saw no point watering down Solomon's offer. Her face went pale. She tried not to think what that experience might be like. She quickly glanced at me and away. She tried to hide her thoughts. I knew she was evaluating me, wondering if I was enough to keep her safe.

"Maybe we should go to the shelters," she said.

She looked me right in the eye without blinking. I knew the question had been asked as a challenge, a test. My shoulders sank.

"If you want to go to the shelters, you can take the car and go," I said.

"You won't come?"

"I thought we agreed we didn't trust the shelters," I said.

"Doesn't this change things?" she asked. "How do we know the shelters are worse than this?"

"Because people with immunity do not need the shelters," I said. "And it's just a gut feeling."

"Any other gut feelings?"

"Yes. Anyone tries to hurt you, and I will decorate our fence with their heads."

She smiled, half amused at my bravado and the other half seeing the severe intent in my eyes, no matter how naive it might've been.

"I'm a joke to you?" I asked.

"Of course not—"

"I will kill anyone who tries to hurt you. You doubt me?"

"You're a killer now?" she asked. "One month ago, you were just—"

"A boy? And I'm still a boy to you, is that it?"

"I didn't say that. You're doing very well."

"Maybe he's trying to scare us into going onto the roads," I said. "Have you thought of that?"

"I haven't thought of that. I'm scared, dammit!"

"Well, you shouldn't be!" I said. "Anyone who breaks into this house is a dead man. I would kill myself if anything happened to you."

She didn't know how to react to that at first.

"You don't know what you're saying."

"Because I'm a boy. Because I don't have children."

"You're not a boy," she said. "I was wrong to insinuate that. You have to remember I was there when you were born! We're both grown-ups. I'm just a little more grown-upper than you.

"But, yes, it's true you don't—didn't—have children. You don't know how much that makes you afraid of danger. I'm sure your dad would say the same thing!"

My dad. How would he be handling this?

"I'm afraid," I said. "I don't know your pain. But I know pain."

"I know."

Dad would have told me a boy doesn't proclaim himself a man. He assumes the mindset and responsibility. I tried to avoid a mental picture of him seeing me lose my temper. Allowing myself to get sweet on Kimberly now seemed a waste of time. I resolved not to lose control again.

"My dad thought it best to stay here," I said. "It's been a while, but it's still too early to know what's happening. I'm staying. I'm not your boss, though. If you want to go, take your van and go. I'll give you some supplies. You'll have the guns. I can draw you a map if you don't know the county roads."

She watched me, curious about my change in mood.

"I would wait at least a week, though," I said. "I'm sure they're waiting in the woods for us to run off."

A painful silence clouded the room. She took a deep breath. I stood and started out of the room.

"I'm going to check the house and fence," I said.

"Don't let them take me alive," she said.

I stopped and watched her.

"I won't let them take you. I promise," I said.

"Don't let them take me alive," she said. "Do you understand?"

I assured her that I understood.

We checked the house for any possible way to break in. Dad had every possible entrance blocked. I couldn't help but think we were overlooking something. Part of Solomon's game was to burrow into my mind, making me think we couldn't be safe and, therefore, must flee.

Being outside or having the windows uncovered was no longer safe. The thought of being stuck inside a dark, stuffy house for God knows how long had me almost too sick to eat dinner.

I suggested we return to our original rooms. Better we're not in the same room. If one of us was caught, the other might have been given a warning.

She didn't argue.

Two Hearts

Amid the stress of those days—the struggle to survive, the threats from Solomon, and the continuing grief of our lost families, I somehow decided that was the perfect time to tell Kimberly I loved her.

By the end of August, it had been two weeks since Solomon's threatening visit. We had gone over the house and property with a fine toothcomb. The fences, gates, and razor wire were good but would never withstand serious assault. Wires could be cut, and a team of men could've made quick work of it. So, we focused on the house.

Thanks to Dad's foresight, we were in good shape. We had weapons, water, ammo, and food. How long it lasted was a mystery, dependent on too many variables. There was only the day-to-day.

We agreed going outside was not a good idea, especially alone. We ran the air conditioning during the day. Electricity still came to the house. My dad had his bills set to auto-pay. I found paperwork on his nightstand relating to the home and accounts. In this time of living in Neverland, I knew obligations would be met for a long while. I hoped it would continue until courts functioned again and I could take proper control of the estate.

We spent two weeks with windows covered and air conditioning blowing part of the time. It was misery.

Kimberly and I sat in the family room on a hotter-than-average night. A pitiful box fan did its best to cool us off. We were drenched in sweat and breathing heavily, not for fun reasons.

"Should I turn on the air conditioning?" she asked.

"We already ran it this afternoon," I said.

"Was that yes or no?" she said.

"It was a statement of fact."

"I don't want statements of fact. I want an answer."

"It's a free country."

"Another statement of fact?"

She might have hit me if she hadn't been suffering heat exhaustion.

"Turn it on or don't. It was your idea to conserve electricity."

She huffed, shook her head, and gave up.

"Want to watch a movie?"

She looked and asked me if I was kidding right then.

"If we're going to burn electricity, let's burn it turning on the god-damn air conditioner!" she said.

The stupidity of the argument hit us both at the same time. We laughed through the heat and sweat.

"We're like an old married couple," she said.

"I sure do love you," I said.

There. It was out. Relief. She didn't hear it as I'd said it. She smiled and turned to look at me, weary and gorgeous.

"I sure do love you too, kid."

"I think I'd like to build something together with you."

"Yeah? I think the kids' Legos are around here somewhere."

I took a deep breath. I was hot, sweating, emotionally frustrated, and in too many ways to count.

"Gave up Legos a while back," I said.

She looked at me, wondering if I was offended. I smiled. No worries.

"I meant nothing by it."

I realized Kimberly was the type of woman who didn't read between the lines. I pushed myself up and walked over to her chair. When she saw I wanted to sit on the coffee table, she moved her feet and let me sit down. I gently took her hand. She looked down at our hands and back up to me. Her face was strained. She squeezed my hand, but more out of anxiety than affection.

"I love you," I said.

Her breathing quickened. She was surprised, which didn't surprise me. I knew an initial rejection was coming. I'd have to say it more than once. But there was something behind her eyes that seemed happy, relieved, that there was a sign of life, of emotion between us.

She opened her mouth several times as if to answer, then changed her mind and remained silent. I smiled, patient, ready to listen. I'd sit back down and turn on a movie if it was a rejection.

After all her stops and starts, she managed to squeeze out, "I . . . uh . . . . wow."

"I wasn't talking about Legos when I said I wanted to build something. I want us to build a life together. It's no accident that you and I are the only survivors. My dad always told me the extraordinary is no accident. We need to pay attention when things like that happen."

She was in complete shock. "I, I, I can't have any more children."

She guffawed at how ridiculous that sounded. It encouraged me because it meant she had already thought of it, wanting me to know what might or might not be possible.

"Not just talking about children," I said. "We've been living in a weird, suspended animation for weeks. This whole thing with these pirates? It's got me thinking. The thought of them hurting you arouses something in me. If I lost you . . . well, let's just say I will die to protect you."

She was in tears now. She clutched my hand with a grip strengthened by warmth and feeling.

"I can't believe this," she said. "Aren't I too old for you?"

"I've aged more than you these past few weeks."

"Your parents were my friends."

"We don't live in that world anymore," I said. "But I'm not about pressure. You can take some time to think about it."

I started to stand, but she pulled me back down.

"I do have great affection for you, Colby," she said. "And I suppose, yes, maybe that has crossed into love. It's been so long since I've been in this position that it's hard for me to recognize it. Here I am, an old lady starting to sag and wrinkle. I look at you, this huge muscular young man, and damn, if I were a college girl again, I'd be ravaging you night and day."

I put my other hand on top of our hands. "I wish you could see yourself through my eyes. I don't see an old lady. I don't see any sagging or wrinkling. I see an incomparable beauty, someone perfectly matched to me.

"Right now, we're living with no past and no future. Just day-to-day same old thing with no growth, no star to steer by. But together, I know we could make a future happen."

"Don't be mad at me for saying this," she said, now crying. "You don't know the pain I'm feeling."

"I was never a parent. I know you told me—"

She shushed me.

"I need to be clear on this. You lost your parents and your sisters. I know how much this has torn you apart, and I'm sorry if I downplayed it earlier," she said. "But to lose children . . ."

She pulled her hand away and buried her face in her hands, sobbing. I felt terrible dredging all of this up, but part of me felt like it was time to plant a flag and take a different direction.

"Losing parents, losing spouses, even losing siblings," she said. "It's different than children. I lost my brother and my parents. That was bad enough. But after losing Lydia and Sebastian, I have to teach myself how to breathe again every morning. You don't know what that's like. I've got nothing left for you. I played my hand, and I'm cashed out. It's all I can do to move. I only smile out of defiance, a sense that I should at least make a go of it because I know they would try to live if they were still here.

"But I gotta be honest with you, Colby. I'm disappointed the beam didn't take me. Right now, I'm just waiting to die so I can be with my family again."

I couldn't think of any way to persuade her, or even if I should. It was best to let it go. I tried.

Her hands relaxed. I let her go. She looked away from me and stared at the giant shutter covering the window. In less stressful times, it would've opened out to a beautiful view of the ocean.

"Do you think we'll survive these pirates?" she asked.

I had thought about that question, examining every possible scenario, wondering which was most likely.

"If they can get into the house, I don't think our odds are good."

She looked at me. "Do you think they can get into the house?"

"I don't see how," I said. "But I'm not my father. There may be something I haven't thought of."

She looked away again. "I see."

I couldn't gauge her reaction. "Does that make you happy or sad?"

She laughed again, covering her eyes with her hands. It was such a beautiful sound. Her mouth bent into the sweetest smile, framed by dimples and perfect symmetry.

It seemed like a good moment to end the night. I stood and stretched, readying to leave. She gave me a strange look as if she didn't want me to leave and stood. In the living room, we stood close enough that we almost touched.

"I'll say this once. If you want to play another hand, I'm your man. I'll take good care of you and protect you. Since I've never loved anyone, I'm all yours for the molding. So, you think about my offer, okay?"

She looked up at me. Her wide, soft brown eyes bored into mine. Her breathing quickened. My heart beat so hard and fast that I worried she would see my chest pounding.

"I will," she said.

I was naive and inexperienced, but Dad always told me a good rule of life, when in doubt, was to go for it. I didn't know what would happen next, but I didn't care to stand there and leave things to chance.

I unbuttoned her beach dress and opened it. She still wore that black one-piece swimsuit that looked like it came from Kohl's or something. I put my hands on her shoulders. It was familiar but safe, not too far out of line. She tilted her chin up to mine and closed her eyes. I leaned down, and our lips touched.

I lost track of how long we kissed. We kissed deeply, passionately. We kissed each other according to our own experience, but after several minutes, we found our own rhythm and unique way. She put her hands on my shoulders. My fingers reached under the straps of her bathing suit. Then, we pulled away from each other at the same time. My thoughts were cloudy, swimming in desire and arousal.

She lowered her hands to my chest and drummed her fingers as if she had remembered something. She backed away from me.

"Very nice," she said. "Very nice."

She smiled at me, confident and at peace. I knew whatever had just happened was right. Time would tell if we could build on it.

"Whew! I am thirsty," she said.

She went to the kitchen and ran the faucet for a glass of water. I could see into the kitchen from where I stood. She looked back at me and smiled. Her beach dress was still unbuttoned. At this point, my senses were heightened. I noticed everything about her—scuffed toenail polish, the curves of her body, and most importantly, the flushed and aroused look on her face, the way her eyelids were partially closed, giving her the sultry look of an old movie star.

It felt like I was being tested. How would she be testing me? I watched her, trying to decipher what exactly was going on. I had told her I loved her. I hadn't exactly proposed marriage, but by telling her I wanted to build for the future, that's exactly what I was implying. She had said no without actually using the word. Suddenly, I had an idea.

I turned to go upstairs. In so doing, I passed behind a stuffed chair whose backrest came up to my navel. I slipped off my gym shorts and stood naked, blocked from her view. I shifted to the side just enough so that when Kimberly looked, she would see the outside edges of my body, but the chair would block the big boys from view.

"I'm going to go upstairs and sleep," I said.

"Okay," she said.

She glanced at me and saw that I was bare but hiding myself, and she gasped. I threw my shorts at her. She caught them. Her eyes were wide in shock, surprise, and puzzlement.

I went upstairs, still blocked by the chair, and entered my room. I stretched out on the covers and waited to see what would happen.

My room and the entire upstairs was dark. The downstairs ambient light went off as Kimberly killed the lights. I heard the soft creak of her tiny feet ascending the stairs. I kept my eyes closed, wanting to be surprised by what came next.

Something landed on my chest. I jumped in surprise. Shadows flitted past my doorway. I lifted her bathing suit off my chest. I heard her voice once she knew I was aware of what she had done.

"I'll be in my room," she said.

I didn't go to her room at night, nor did she come to me. I didn't realize it then, but I had been testing her. And because we had the connection

I'd hoped, she had tested me right back. Both of us passed the test. We were willing and able to take each other physically. We had also proven to each other that there was more we wanted.

I folded her swimsuit and crept to the doorway to set it in the hallway. There I found my shorts. Kimberly's room was further down the hall. The lights were off, but I knew she was waiting.

I put my shorts back on and returned to bed. That night was the most peaceful sleep I'd had since everything changed.

INVADERS

I remember a professor telling me that a person can sense an incoming punch, even if it's a sucker punch and they aren't looking. I don't know who volunteered for tests like that, but if you watch in slow motion, even a guy getting blindsided will cringe away from the incoming blow at the last minute.

That's the only way I can explain the timing when Solomon's men came for us. It was the very next night after Kimberly and I had kissed. It was no accident at all, in a spiritual sense. We endured for two weeks after Solomon's threat without kissing or touching. Only when it was the day before what might have been our last night alive did we both feel the urge to connect.

They came through the storage room. If that sounds like an audacious plan on their part, it was because they didn't know what room they were coming into. They had tunneled to the house from the northern woods, taking the aforementioned two weeks. They had knocked the foundation bricks in. We didn't hear it because they smashed in during a thunderstorm three nights before. Luckily, all the weapons had been moved out of the safe and into our rooms.

I spent many college nights watching horror films. They relieve stress, give me mindless entertainment, and put my mind on other things. I always wondered what encountering a Jason or a Michael Myers creeping through your house would be like. After the night the pirates came, I no longer had to wonder.

If Kimberly hadn't managed to kick my bedroom wall with her heel as they dragged her away, I might never have known what had happened and never had enough warning to fight against the men charging into my room. I wouldn't have awakened at all.

As it was, a thump jolted me awake just in time to see two large, bare-chested men rushing at my bed. I sat up to fight when one of them dove at me. His tackle sent both of us rolling off the bed and into the wall.

He was big. Not as big as me, but big enough to rock me hard. He had smacked his head as hard as I did. I tried to shake out the dizziness as I got to my feet. The second man came running around the bed with his fist cocked and ready to put me out. I ducked away and drove my right fist hard into his shoulder. I could tell I had struck a nerve by the way he screamed. This allowed me to run around the bed and out the door.

All of this happened in fractions of a second. Kimberly had been dragged downstairs. I was sick with fear over what would be done to her, what might already be happening to her. I entered the hallway, and the first guy slammed me against the wall.

I never had proper training on how to fight. I'd always been a big kid, and bullies never bothered me. Football players avoided fights because everyone was muscled and strong; nobody wanted to risk injury. But these guys, I could tell, not only knew how to fight, they knew how to kill and were comfortable doing it. I caught the glint of steel from the knives hanging from their belts. They didn't draw them, and I knew why. Solomon had promised me that if I rejected his offer, they would make me watch what was done to Kimberly. There would never be a more desperate fight. I remembered my promise to Kimberly not to let her be taken and fought on with desperation.

I grabbed my attacker by the head and twisted hard. His neck didn't break—that's a movie thing—but it did force him straight to the ground. It's a move I pulled on a defensive end or two to get into the ground quickly. You can't do it too often because your chances of getting flagged are fifty-fifty.

The move worked as I had hoped. He collapsed to his chest. I drove my knee into his back with the full force of my 235 pounds. He let out a croaking gasp as the wind rushed out of him. By then, the second man ran at me from the bedroom. He was fleet-footed, moving fast at me like an all-conference safety. I surprised him by closing the distance and flattening him like the all-conference (alternate) tight end I was.

They were dazed and hurt for a moment. I ran back into the bedroom and grabbed my revolver from under my pillow. I should have shot the two men while lying there, but I was inexperienced. All I could think of was getting to Kimberly as soon as possible. I ran down into the living room and froze.

Two more goons held Kimberly in the living room. One held her in front of him—one arm around her throat, the other holding her hands together behind her back. Only his face was visible above her right shoulder. The second gripped her hair and held a knife to her throat.

Her eyes were wet and red. Moonlight came in through the windows. They had removed the shutters. The way they had violated Kimberly had me seeing red. I would kill with my teeth if I had to. And this is only the beginning of what they had planned for her. But for now, I had to think.

"Go ahead, mate!" said the goon holding Kimberly.

I heard thumping behind me. The two men who had attacked me had recovered and now stood behind me. We were trapped. Kimberly was helpless. My two attackers stood behind me, knives out and ready to start it up again. I held the revolver at my side. It was visible, but the four invaders didn't seem too scared. They knew they had the upper hand. So did I. So did Kimberly.

I had one shot, if that. Once I pulled the trigger, they would jump me and start a nightmare beyond imagining.

"Here's what's gonna happen, mate," said the goon. "We're going to move this show out into the moonlight. Our fun and games always look better in the moonlight. We're well-practiced, and it's our pleasure to entertain you!"

The other men laughed. I heard the lust and insanity in their voices.

"Now, you open that back door and lead the way. You're free to run if you want, but you won't be able to outrun the screamin'."

He said it so matter of factly, like he was just here to sand the deck or check the roof. After I hesitated, he nodded at the goon with the knife. Knife-man grabbed a handful of her swimsuit and cut it open from her navel and through the neckline.

"Sharp, innit?" the goon asked.

I focused on Kimberly's eyes. She was terrified, as was I, but there was something else in the look she gave me. A reminder. A reminder of my promise not to let her be taken. With a broken heart, I realized where my shot had to go. They would never expect me to put a bullet through Kimberly. Hell, the bullet would probably kill the goon behind her. The shock might paralyze the others long enough for me to fight it if I had the willpower.

The goon holding Kimberly finally noticed my gun.

"Drop it, mate," he said.

I was out of options. Killing Kimberly was the only heroic thing I could do. I would shoot her, and they would kill me. At least it would be quick.

Kimberly suddenly went limp. The goon holding her struggled to keep her dead weight upright. The Knife-man cackled.

"She can't handle the pressure!" he said. "Let's see if she's really out of it."

He reached for her breast, and I shot him in the throat.

Time froze. Kimberly's goon dropped her. He reached for a pistol in his belt. My two goons stood still in shock. Knife-man dropped to the floor, making a horrible sound. Kimberly rolled away toward the back curtains, and I knew she had faked it. Her goon saw the same thing and growled as he pulled his pistol to shoot her.

I fired at him and missed, but it made him duck and gave her time to ready the AR-15 stashed behind the curtains.

My goons finally reacted. The short one was too slow. I shot him dead through the navel. He screamed and fell. The tall one swung at me, knife in hand, and I grabbed his wrist. He seized my gun hand before I could aim. We struggled that way for a second, trying to kick at each other. He was too tall for me to overpower him from above. Instead, we pushed against each other's wrists, our muscles and arms shaking as we each gave everything, knowing mistakes were death.

Kimberly's attacker panicked when she aimed her rifle at him. It was just enough time for her to switch off the safety and blast a round through his thigh. He screamed like a banshee and fired recklessly. The combined screaming and explosions in an enclosed space drove me to insanity. One of his wild rounds hit my opponent in the hip. He crumpled to the floor, which allowed me to put two shots into the top of his head.

The talking goon fired his pistol dry without hitting either of us. Only Kimberly's goon was still alive. She sat in the corner, aiming her rifle at the man and shaking.

"Are you okay?" I asked.

She shook her head yes. "You?"

"Fine."

Somehow, we had triumphed. The goon clutched his destroyed thigh and breathed heavily. He gritted his teeth and watched us. I turned on the lights. Kimberly's face was dark red. Her chest nearly spilled out of her slashed bathing suit. I turned to the goon.

"Did you hit her?"

Even though he was beaten, what I had seen done to Kimberly left me in no mood for mercy. She saw darkness color my face.

'Colby, calm down," she said. "It's over."

I'm not proud of what came next. So many thoughts fought for supremacy at that moment. Punishment was required. A message needed to be sent to Solomon, his men, and anybody with similar ideas. For that reason, I stomped on his thigh. Not to kill him. But to torture him. He screamed in pain and beat on the floor with his fists.

"Colby!"

I grabbed him by his collar and dragged him to the deck. My strength surged so hard I would have been first-team all-American if I'd summoned it on the field. Kimberly followed.

I dragged him over the deck, through the grass, past the gate, and onto the beach. Kimberly stopped on the deck, still holding the rifle.

I released the goon on the sand.

"Is it true you've done this to dozens of people?" I asked.

He didn't answer. I stomped his thigh again. He screamed again, hopefully loud enough for Solomon to hear. Kimberly admonished me again.

"Yeah, I guess we did," he said.

"Why?" I asked.

He was quiet for a while.

"Fine," I said.

I tucked the pistol into my shorts. He had a knife in a belt sheath. I took it out.

"I can promise you I'll learn everything," I said.

He watched me warily when a hole exploded out of his head. I spun around, fearing we'd overlooked someone. Kimberly stood there with a smoking rifle. She'd killed him.

The sun was over the eastern forests by the time we got the blood cleaned up in the house and put back together. Exhaustion doesn't even begin to describe how tired we were. We sat together on the couch when we were finished. My arm was around her, and she nestled close. We were too tired to sleep. She still wore her slashed bathing suit. My shorts were covered in blood. We must have been a sight.

"They didn't rape me," she said.

That startled me.

"I'm sure you're wondering," she said. "Our would be, eventually."

"That's good," I said. "That's real good. Well, you sure as hell violated that guy."

She snorted laughter. It got quiet again for a minute. She toyed with the mangled fabric of her suit.

"Did you see my boobs?" she asked. "They spilled out in the fracas. Did you see?"

"It was too dark. Dammit."

"You sure? Didn't sneak a peek?"

"If I had caught you coming out of the shower, yes. I might sneak a peek in those circumstances," I said. "But what happened out here? No. No peeks were sneaked."

She took a deep breath.

"Good," she said. "Because you don't get to see them until the honeymoon."

Once again, I was startled into silence.

"That shut you up, didn't it?" she said.

"How are we getting to a honeymoon?" I asked. "Are you proposing to me?"

"Oh, hell no. I'm old-fashioned. It's the man's job to do the proposing," she said. "It's just that based on what you told me earlier, I assumed you'd be getting around to it."

"I thought you didn't have any more cards to play."

"I guess I got one or two more up my sleeve."

A fantastic golden light came in from the east windows.

"Is that too hokey and weird for you?" she asked.

"No way," I said. "I'd like that. I want to get married."

"I was thinking about Lydia last night," she said. "She was sick as a child, in case you don't remember. I spent a lot of time at the hospital. She kept such a good attitude. She was so positive, believing that it would all get better. And it did. There were times when I didn't think I could go on. I don't know how I did, but I did.

"But she got better. That's the point. And even though she and Sebastian and Philip are gone. It's still worth it, isn't it?"

"Yes," I said.

There was no doubt in my mind.

"Then I say we play another hand," she said. "Let's have faith in the future. If the future only gives us one more day, I want to be playing a hand."

"Kimberly," I said. "Will you marry me?"

"Absolutely."

I didn't know how to celebrate the moment. So, we just sat there. I kissed her.

"So, how we can pull this off?" I asked. "It would be dangerous to go out and try and find a church that was still open."

"Church? I want a chapel with an Elvis impersonator," she said. "If you can't find that, I will improvise in a way God will approve of."

For the first time in a couple of months, I felt hope.

We still had some unpleasant duties to perform, although we didn't let it damper enthusiasm for our engagement. I had to fill in the tunnel dug by the pirates and seal up the hole in the basement storage room. The cinder blocks weren't broken, merely bashed in. I reset them with the mortar that Dad had in the garage. It took three days to hide the tunnel to my satisfaction.

We hung the dead men's clothes on the wrought-iron back fence. I took their bodies to sea—far from where we'd buried our loved ones—and dumped them.

Solomon had not been among them.

A DIVINE PROMISE

O ur electricity went off the afternoon of our engagement. It never came back. Water continued to flow, though. We laughed it off, having expected it sooner or later. We had gone electricity-free as much as we could to prepare for the moment—no more heat or air-conditioning. Dad had a gas-powered generator in the garage. He showed me how to connect it to the house and flip the transfer switch to draw power from the generator. We had a small supply of gas, but we saved it for emergencies, checking TV broadcasts, and super-hot afternoons. A box of batteries sat in the storage room for small appliances like radios.

Thoughts of Solomon, where he was, and what he had planned for us were the immediate concern. If he hadn't seen me dumping the bodies of his men into the ocean, he certainly was aware that his men had not returned and that his raid had gone wrong. We had yet to hear the last of him. It added one more undercurrent of danger to the lives we were trying to lead. We never spoke of the attack again. In hindsight, I realized that Solomon personified the evil chaos that had descended upon nature and our loved ones.

Getting married? The idea seemed so ridiculous that it was the only option for those who refused to give up and insisted on standing firm against the headwinds and steering themselves according to a reckless, foolish faith.

We sat outside and talked about the details. First week of September. It was cool that day. Nice ocean breeze. Cloudless and perfect, but we had to break out long-sleeved shirts.

"Is there a functioning church nearby?" she asked.

"There's a small country church in the village," I said. "Dad said the area was overrun, looted, and burned."

"I wonder if any pastors survived."

"I think so. Probably. But how would we contact one?" I asked. "We really shouldn't leave the property."

"Magistrates aren't doing weddings, you think?" she asked.

We laughed.

"We have no family to give us away," she said. "No friends to bear witness. Wow. You're all I have? I might need to think this through."

"I checked Dad's Bible. Did you know there's nothing in the Bible about how to do the ceremony?" I asked.

"I think I did know that."

"It's a covenant," I said, like it was a profound insight.

"A covenant? Really?"

She leaned forward, hand on her chin.

"You're messing with me," I said. "Anyway, it's a divine promise. We can make a divine promise, just the two of us. God will be watching."

"He's the most important witness."

"It will be legal."

"Divinely legal," she said.

"I say we do it right now."

She gave me that big, beaming smile. It was so nice to have it back.

"I'll ask one more time," she said. "Are you sure this is what you want to do?"

"Never been more sure of anything."

She smiled and sat back.

"How about you?" I asked. "There's danger. Things we can't see yet."

"Crossing this threshold will weave our hearts together in a way that will shatter you if it's ever broken in any way."

"I know," I said. "I realize you have a viewpoint I can't understand."

She removed the wedding ring that Philip had put on her finger many years ago. She was somber but did not cry. She smiled as she held it in her palm and looked at it. I was silent, not entirely sure what was unfolding.

She looked up from the ring and at me. There was no hesitation in her eyes, no sign that she wished things had turned out differently so that Philip was spared instead of me.

"When Philip and I took our vows," she said. "We vowed to stay together 'until death do us part.' And now death has parted us. Whatever kind of vow you and I take, it's to the death. Do you understand?"

"I understand," I said.

"But I don't want the word death in our vows," she said. "I'll leave it up to you to create something different."

"I can do that."

"And hurry. We should do this before nightfall."

Time was a precious commodity; you never knew how much was left in the account. It was best to spend it as needed. There were no points for saving it.

She wanted to pretty herself up, which meant digging out a summer dress she had brought. I went on the boat and caught fresh fish for a nice dinner. I had Dad's fishing guide and his very expensive rod and reel. The fishing guide had pictures of fish to avoid if I was looking for something to eat. I was out on the ocean longer than intended. I didn't want to return empty-handed.

I caught an eel and a small shark. Both of those went back. The fishing guide said those were a no-no. I gave it one more try and brought in a 5-pound tuna. I was delighted until I checked the guide and found out that I shouldn't bring in tuna because they were endangered. Well, their days of being endangered were now over, so I brought it in.

It'd been a while since my mom showed me how to clean and gut a fish, and it was very messy—Kimberly turned away and left to change clothes—but I managed to get two nice, big fillets out of it. She brought up canned potatoes and a can of mac & cheese. I cooked on the gas grill.

I went up to my room and pawed through my suitcase. Luckily, Mom had told me to bring something at least semi-nice to wear in case we went to an upscale restaurant. For me in those days, nice meant an above-average plain black T-shirt and dark blue jeans with no holes in them.

Kimberly was still in her room. I went to the beach, thinking I should prepare, wishing I had thought of this earlier. I rolled up my pant legs and strolled along the water, thinking.

A pile of driftwood, one of many dotting the beach, caught my eye. I stood and stared at it for a moment. If I used my imagination, some of the hunks of logs and branches, worn so smooth by the ebbing and flowing of the tide, had an almost human-like appearance.

I jogged to the garage for the spade, then returned to the driftwood. I picked through the driftwood, choosing pieces that resembled our family members. I had to stretch my imagination to a level I'd never used before. The resemblance was good in most cases.

I arranged them according to size. There were four for my family — the tallest one, about 3 feet tall, for Dad, Mom, Madison, and finally, Sophia. After so many weeks of thinking my emotions had reached their cruising altitude, everything rose again. I didn't cry, not that I was holding it back, just a twisting of the heart and tears briefly spilling over.

I chose the best spot to stand together and have a modest ceremony. I dug four holes in the wet sand on the right side, facing the sea. I briefly held each piece of wood before placing them in the holes and burying them standing up. In my mind and with my heart, I reached out to each of them in heaven, hoping they could read my mind and feel my feelings. It was the only way I could ask their permission for what we were about to do.

I patted the sand around the base of each piece of wood until I had four smooth logs jutting out a foot or two. My family. My witnesses.

I dug three holes for Kimberly's family but left the smooth driftwood lined up on the sand.

I returned to the deck and started on dinner. The grill heated up quickly. I put the fillets on the grill on one side and a couple of small saucepans with the potatoes and pasta on the other. As I stood watching the food sizzle and bubble, I realized I had nothing to give Kimberly on her wedding day. No stores were open. She wouldn't be expecting anything. But there had to be something.

I walked around the wild grass to see if there was a flower I could use. Along the fence, I found a plant with a tall winding stem sprouting pink, white, and purple bell-shaped flowers along its length. Foxglove, Kimberly would later tell me. She also jokingly told me it was an invasive species. All I saw was a pretty flower. Curious how our perspective shapes our perceptions.

I picked a three-foot length of the plant and wound it around into a makeshift crown. Then I returned to the grill, tended to dinner, and waited for Kimberly.

A few minutes later, she stepped onto the deck wearing a teal summer dress with yellow flowers. Her shoulders were bare. She had managed to get her hair styled despite having no electricity. She stood still on the deck for a few seconds, hand on her hip, enjoying my reaction.

"What do you think?" she asked.

It was difficult to process how beautiful she was, especially in the context of the craziness that our lives had become.

"I think you're marrying up, my lady," I said.

She giggled, a sound that made everything even more perfect.

"Oh, brother," she said. "Are you Lord of the Manor now?"

"Yes, I'm glad you clean up well. Now I can say you are truly worthy of me."

She rolled her eyes and joined me at the grill.

"How's dinner coming?" she asked.

"Looks like everything is done. It can warm for a second."

I led her through the gate and out onto the beach. We held hands and strolled ankle-deep into the water. The waves tickled my ankles, but the water felt perfect. The breeze was warm and gentle. Birds passed high overhead, indifferent to the changes below. They were too high to tell what they were, but their presence gave me a calming sense of grander things than worry and fear.

She spotted the driftwood. She glanced at me, curious, then studied my display again. It didn't take her long to figure out what these pieces of wood represented.

"You need witnesses at a wedding, and I know we should have our family's approval."

She looked at the three pieces of driftwood lying on their side. "Oh, wow."

"I'm sure my family would approve of you," I said.

"I know," she said. "I approve of you."

She tenderly placed the smaller pieces of driftwood into the holes I made. She caressed them so sweetly before lowering them down. She swept the sand into the hole with her hands to stand them upright. She held the large piece of wood before her for close to a minute. She quickly kissed it and stood it up next to the others.

Now we had witnesses.

We faced each other. I could've absorbed the contours of her face for hours. She didn't seem older than me then. Despite the constant anxiety and trauma we went through, she did not appear aged, as one might expect. There was something within her that was good and alive and could not be defeated.

I had been to several weddings. I took for granted what spectacular events they were, all the fine clothing, flowers, and sacred music. It overwhelmed me when I was a kid sitting in the pews, bearing witness to it. It seemed strange not to have all those things for my wedding.

Then I looked around. I spent so much time living in fear that I had tuned out all the good surrounding me. It was all here — the sea, mountains, the beach, the incomparable beauty of the most perfect woman I ever met. It was an ideal place for two people–isolated by fate, drawn by God— to make a simple promise in the middle of the grandest pageant of all.

Neither of us was the kind to use as many words as possible. It was part of how we related. We said what we had to say and were done. So it was that day. I promised to love her and give my life for her, if necessary. I remembered her wish not to have the phrase "till death do us part" in our vows. I ended my promise by saying:

"Until we sleep."

She smiled at those words.

"Perfect," she said.

She repeated a similar promise to me. When it was done, she also said:

"Until we sleep."

We asked God to look down upon us as we made that promise and asked for his help to endure.

Dinner was wonderful. The sky grew cloudy and dark. We didn't mind. The cool air was nice. When it started to rain, though, it was time to go inside.

I swept her up into my arms. I jostled her up and down a bit to show off how strong I was and how light she was in my arms. She laughed. Then I carried her inside, taking my time. We kissed along the way.

I carried her up the stairs and into my room in the tower. That's where I set her down. We stood together at the window, watching and listening as the rain began to pour. We were nervous, not because we wanted to avoid what was coming next but because that feeling of anticipation had seemed forever out of reach until today.

It was there, in my bed in the tower, with the windows open, that everything started anew. The cool mist wafting into the room was all we wore. It was my first time, but she was a good and patient teacher. I was a fast learner and an even better innovator.

The rain turned into a storm, but we barely took notice. We outlasted the storm. We outlasted the moon. We outlasted sunrise.

I took that as a good omen.

LILIANA

There was nothing to prepare me for married life like this. I knew plenty of married people. Some were happy, some not. Most occupied an odd neutral zone where days just went by for them. My parents had the best marriage I'd ever seen. They argued sometimes, but there was a centering peace that I knew I wanted with my future wife.

Kimberly told me we were free to make our thing whatever we wanted. She often referred to her marriage to Philip as a way of sparing us hardship and conflict she already knew how to avoid. I wasn't offended. I had thought about how Philip's memory might complicate things. What if being married again made her miss Philip more than it brought her close to me?

I needn't have worried. There was much to learn from Kimberly's experience. She had a couple of decades on me, after all. Foolish to pretend that wasn't the case. No matter how hard we tried, there was still a road bump. Minor things arise when both people pull the curtain aside and let someone into their most intimate spaces.

The wild grass around the house faded to yellow toward the middle of September. Fall would soon be upon us. Trees would turn color and shed their leaves. I didn't care to imagine the bleak, barren forests glowering down upon us when that time came. That was for another time, far off and waiting.

In those days, Kimberly and I wandered through the golden grass. We stretched out blankets and made love as the radiant waves surrounded us. She sang to me. I never knew she was so good at it. We had plenty of laughs in those days. Time paused. Nightmares from Solomon's goons went away. Hurts rolled out with the tide. God smiled upon us. In those golden fields, we had everything.

After a week or so as lively newlyweds, we sat in the sun side-by-side on our loungers.

"So, where do you want to go on our honeymoon?" I asked.

She looked at me, puzzled until she saw I was being facetious.

"I want to go to a beautiful house in the middle of nowhere, right along the ocean," she said.

"I can manage that," I said. "Too bad we don't have a resort to go to where we could cavort and have a fully stocked buffet in the evenings."

"The grass is always greener," she said.

She laughed and rolled her eyes. Then she looked back at me again and winked.

"I have an idea you might like," she said.

She stood up, doffed her dress, and tossed it on the lounger. She wore nothing underneath. That would create more laundry. She did that hands-on-her-hips thing she was so good at and smiled.

"I say we take a honeymoon from all this restrictive fabric," she said.

My shorts were already off before she finished the sentence.

"And how long is this going to last?" I asked.

She shrugged, and our itinerary for the rest of the day was set.

It was set for several days. We were a couple of newlyweds at a beach-side home, wearing absolutely nothing and falling upon each other whenever one or both of us had the urge, which was often. We never talked about it, but I realized that not only did making love to Kimberly complete my soul, it was the only respite I had from the lingering pain of losing my family.

Worries were few in those days, but we kept watch and kept the place secure. We checked in on the TV at least once a day to see if there were any new instructions. In the early days, authorities had claimed they expected order to be restored in two weeks. Always that number. Two weeks. Two weeks until the military defeats the invaders. Two weeks until power is restored. Only a two-week stay at the shelter until people could return home. Looking in on the emergency broadcast became a tedious chore. There was never any news—just the same instruction to report to the shelters. I wondered how many shelters there were. Did they keep expanding? At what point were the shelters full?

The sheer numbers of the dead were staggering. Statistics were oddly shoehorned into the emergency broadcasts. My best guess is that it was done to stoke fear. If the number of dead were valid, there were only a small number of survivors. It's odd they still called for survivors. Only stragglers like us had to be left, and we couldn't be worth worrying about. Something didn't add up. But there was no way to know then what the truth was.

We discussed what we might do if refugees came. The house had plenty of room. There were plenty of food supplies. And we had a moral obligation to do so. But no one came.

Sometimes, we lay in bed in the tower with our limbs tangled together, talking about our lives' unbelievable turn. I like to picture angels with flaming swords standing on the path to our house, forbidding anyone from interrupting us.

In quiet moments, I enjoyed the feel of her skin, her hair, the sound of her voice, and the rhythms of her breathing. Unspoken between us was the realization that there was no escape. Had God put this plan into motion? Had he allowed some other entity to do so for His purposes? I didn't believe then or now that it was all random chance. Soon—measured by days, years, or decades—it would all be over.

But those were constant worries that had haunted lovers throughout history. The strongest memory, the most aching feeling I carry from those days, is the romantic, loving innocence of frolicking naked in the sun, cut off from the horrors of the world, enjoying our own personal Eden together. It was a rare thing.

We slept well when we slept. Amazing how life had descended into such horror, only to rise again to love and beauty, at least in our tiny corner of the world. Before, I would close my eyes at night, wondering if I would wake up the next day. We never shook the feeling that each night might bring a new threat that would take one of us. But after Kimberly became my wife, I slept soundly and woke contented.

We had defied the new horrors of the world, and whatever pulled the levers of that new horror would not tolerate rebellion without an answer.

We heard a woman calling for help. At first, we thought it might've been a bird or some animal that wandered near the fence. It'd been so long since we had heard the voice of another human being it took us some moments to recognize it.

We heard it again.

"That's a woman's voice," Kimberly said.

I listened. She called out again, sounding urgent.

"It's coming from the front," I said.

The first thing we had to do was rush inside and get dressed. I jumped into my gym shorts and unlocked and removed the barricade from the front door. Kimberly stepped into her dress as I looked through the crack in the door.

She looked to be in her late teens or early twenties. A high school senior or a college freshman. It could've been somebody from one of my classes. She had long, straight blonde hair, blue eyes, and a curvy, athletic build. She saw me looking out the window.

"Oh, thank God," she said. "Can you please help me?"

Kimberly joined me at the door. I wondered how she would react to seeing a pretty young thing at the gate.

"Oh, the poor dear," she said. "Is she okay? How on earth did she make it out here by herself?"

You can see why Kimberly was so easy to love. Her first thought was sympathy, not jealousy.

"Let's get our rifles," I said. "Just in case. This could be a setup."

"Right," she said. "How do you want to handle this?"

"I'll go and talk to her," I said. "You cover me. You see anything fishy, you shoot."

I stepped out onto the front porch.

"Are you alone?" I asked.

"Yes!" she said. "I just need a place to stay. I got away from these guys. I don't think they're following. Oh God, will you please help me?"

"I'm speaking to anyone hiding in the trees," I said. "Step forward right now. If you try sneaking around, you'll be shot. Step forward now."

She looked around, confused. No one came out of the woods. I kept the rifle level as I walked to the gate, looking carefully into the trees to see if anyone hid. I was almost at the gate when I fired two shots to the girl's left, aimed right, and fired another two shots. She screamed, covered her ears, and closed her eyes as I watched for any movement in the woods. There was none.

"What's your name?" I asked.

"Liliana," she said.

"I'm Colby," I said. "This is my house. I don't mean to sound un-friendly, but please be on your best behavior."

"Of course," she said.

"We had to deal with some not-nice people," I said. "Do you under-stand what I mean?'"

She swallowed a lump. "Yes, I do."

I unlocked both padlocks, pulled the gate open, and waved her through. I told her to head to the front door. I closed the gate and secured the locks.

It was strange to have somebody else in the house after we had been alone, the two of us, for nearly two months. Liliana entered and looked around as I locked the door and returned the barricade. She and Kim-berly said hello. Everyone kept their distance from each other.

There were so many questions we had for each other. We all under-stood that no matter how different the details may be, we had all come down the same path — fear, worry, death of loved ones.

Kimberly was better at small talk. People had harrowing stories then, so it wasn't wise to make them talk about their ordeals immediately. I took the opportunity to give Liliana a once-over. She was shorter than Kimberly, which means she was still above average height for a woman. I could tell by the contours of her thighs and shoulders that she had spent time in the weight room, an athlete of some kind. A battered tote bag hung from her shoulder.

"Liliana, I don't mean any offense, but we're going to have to search your bag," I said. "And the rest of you, too."

She looked carefully at Kimberly and then at me.

"Do you mind if your mom does it?" she asked.

Kimberly snickered, unsurprised.

"This is Kimberly," I said. "And she's my wife."

"Oh . . ." She looked from her to me and back again. "Sorry about that."

"Not a problem," Kimberly said.

I held my hand out for her bag. She reluctantly handed it over. I held it open and looked through it. All I was looking for was a blade or a pistol. She had some personal effects in there, but nothing dangerous.

Kimberly searched the girl's person as discreetly as she could. Liliana wore spandex shorts and a sports bra under a tank top and flip-flops. She was not exactly dressed for life on the run. It didn't leave many places to hide a knife.

"I know you don't trust me," Liliana said. "But I'm desperate. Normally, I wouldn't stop at all. I don't have any weapons. I hope you're good people."

"We're good people," Kimberly said. "Just don't get weird on us, and you're free to stay as long as you need to. Are you hungry?"

"Starving," Liliana said.

We took her to the deck for a fancy feast of canned lasagna. She tried to eat in a civilized manner, but she was famished. Judging by the look of her, she wasn't anywhere near starvation. But it doesn't take long for the tummy to start growling from hunger and anxiety.

"My mom used to get this for me and my sister," Liliana said. "It wasn't my favorite, but it's the best thing ever."

Kimberly and I exchanged glances. It was the second time Liliana had referred to Kimberly in a matronly way. The first time was understandable. I caught a look in Kimberly's eye that told me she didn't think the second time was an accident.

SEDUCTION

We camped on the deck most of the afternoon until dusk. Liliana told us her story. We asked questions, and she directed all her answers at me no matter who asked them. She was being polite and tried hard not to do anything that might make us kick her out. I'm sure she was also evaluating us, wondering if we were the type of people still holding on to what was normal behavior or if we had gone to some version of the dark side like so many others.

"So, Liliana, how did you get here?" I asked. "We may as well share our stories."

"My family went to the shelters in the early days," she said. "When we first got there, it looked like one of those places from the movies where they herd everybody up after a disaster. I couldn't believe it was real. Everyone stayed in these barracks, like the Army or something. There were dividers and stuff so each family could have some privacy. We had beds, a couple of chairs, and a table. We had to share the bathrooms and the showers, though."

"How was the food?" Kimberly asked.

Liliana answered to me.

"I liked to go to the cafeteria. They had a lot of good stuff there. It wasn't like the school type of cafeteria food, you know? But they had really good stuff like cheeseburgers, scrambled eggs, spaghetti and meatballs."

"So you were there with your family, and it wasn't all that bad?" I asked.

"The camp itself? No, it wasn't all that bad."

"So you're living a good life, generally speaking, at this shelter," I said. "But one day, you're in the camp, and the next day, you're not there anymore. Why is that?"

She considered her answer for a second, looking at Kimberly, then back to me and down at her feet.

"I should have just stayed in the barracks and read my books," she said. "But I like to get out and walk around. We were free to move around to most places. A few parts were restricted, but only a few.

"It's just that I started noticing that with all the buses coming, there always seemed to be the same number of people around me."

"They kept bringing people into the shelter, but the population wasn't growing," Kimberly said.

"Yes, that's right," she said to me.

"They were doing something to the people once they were there?" I asked. "Moving them to other shelters?"

"Not to other shelters. From the camps to alien bases."

Kimberly and I exchanged a wide-eyed look. Liliana smirked, enjoying how shocked we were.

"I made friends with one of the guards there," she said. "I got him to spill some secrets. He told me people with A-positive blood were being brought to the shelters to be taken elsewhere. I don't know where."

"How did you get them to tell you all of this?" I asked.

"It wasn't hard," she said with a devilish grin.

"So you escaped somehow?" I asked.

"I told my family about it," she said. "My dad tried to tell the Commander that he wanted to take his family and leave. Turns out it's the 'check in but you don't check out' kind of place. They took my family away while I was with my soldier boy. I never saw them again."

I glanced at Kimberly, who was watching Liliana in a way that showed she either didn't believe her story or didn't believe she was distraught by how things had turned out.

"Anyway, I knew they'd come for me next, so I asked my soldier boy to help me get out. And he did."

"Where was this camp located?" I asked.

"Somewhere south of Seattle is all I know for sure."

"And you made it down here on foot?" Kimberly asked.

"I ran marathons in college," Liliana said to me. "I ran when it was safe to do so. If I saw somebody on the road, I would hide in the ditch or the trees."

"What about food?" I asked.

"I took some stuff from the camp with me," she said. "I found the path going up to your house. I almost turned back after I saw the burned-out truck in the ditch. I figured some warlords or people who knew how to fight back lived here. I stuck into the woods along the fence line and watched you for several days."

She laughed and gave us both a sly look.

"You two had your own little Garden of Eden going here. Both of you were strutting around naked everywhere."

Kimberly didn't give her the pleasure of a reaction. So, Liliana knew Kimberly wasn't my mother.

"You have the life," she said. "Anyway, what you had here together looked so inviting, and I was so desperate that I thought maybe I could join you. Sorry if I interfered. I mean, I can do the nudist thing, too, if that's your deal."

I chuckled, more embarrassed than Kimberly that we had been spied upon. "It's not our 'deal,' really. We're enjoying some time of peace.

"Well, is it okay if I stay with you guys?" she asked. "I mean, I won't interfere in your marriage or anything. I'll pull my weight. You can trust me. I'm no threat to anyone!"

"Of course you can stay," Kimberly said.

Liliana kept her eyes on me, but I remained silent until she turned to look at Kimberly. She was going to have to acknowledge Kimberly's authority in this house. I would only trust Liliana once she did.

"But we'll have to barricade you in your room at least for a while," Kimberly said. "It's nothing personal. The reason it's nothing personal is because we don't know you. We had some bad experiences."

Liliana glanced at me to see if I would confirm those rules.

"The door will be barricaded," I said. "But you can open the shutters on your window to let some air in. Just know that if you crawl out the window, there's no getting back into the house unless we let you in."

"Okay, okay," she said. "I'll do whatever you say. I'm serious. I want to settle down and live. I won't be any trouble."

"Good to hear," I said. "Then we shouldn't have to take these measures for long."

Kimberly stood up. "It's starting to get dark. What say we go inside, play a game or two, get to know each other more, and stop talking about serious stuff."

We spent the evening playing board games. We talked and laughed about the old days and how silly all the old worries seemed after all we'd been through.

When Liliana was ready for bed, we showed her to her room. I set a barricade across the door and secured it with a padlock.

"Good night!" I said.

"Good night!" she called from behind the door.

"Good night, Liliana!" Kimberly said.

Silence.

Later, Kimberly and I lay beside each other in bed, catching our breath.

"So, what do you think of her?" Kimberly asked.

"She doesn't like you very much," I said.

"That much is obvious. What do you think her angle is?"

"I don't know," I said. "But she has an angle."

"Do you believe her story?" Kimberly asked.

I shrugged. "I'm in no place to question it. We've been suspicious of those shelters since the beginning. I was doing the math in my head earlier. She said buses and trucks were coming and going. Do you know how we keep hearing the sounds of truck motors? On the other side of Blackjack Hill? What if something creepy is going on over there?"

Kimberly thought about that. She stared at the ceiling and idly drew circles on her skin with her fingertips.

"Well, her story is probably accurate, but I don't trust her motives," she said. "And she's already making moves on you, strutting around in skimpy clothes, waving her ass around. You're a good-looking, studly guy, so maybe you're used to this approach, but know that's exactly what she's doing."

I opened my mouth to speak.

"And don't ask me if I'm jealous," she said. "I've worked very hard to get control of my emotions—all of them. If you decide to run off with her, go. Don't drag it out. Don't make excuses and rationalizations. Just do what you want, and if you choose to leave, I will forget you ever existed."

"Whoa, whoa, whoa," I said. "Take it easy. Yes, she's young and beautiful and has a rockin' body. Okay? But I bet everything on you. Just remember that."

She looked over at me and smiled. "That's what I figured you'd say. But I just wanted to clear the air."

"Well, I might be young, but I'm not that easily distracted. Besides, it would take four of her boobs to equal one of yours."

"Oh? That's the deciding factor, is it?"

"Well, it certainly doesn't hurt."

Near lunchtime the next day, the three of us went down to the beach to enjoy some sun and surf. It was unseasonably warm for that time of year. The breeze was light and perfect. Liliana wasted no time stripping naked and running into the water. She looked back for our reaction. We were surprised, but shock was an emotion we lost a long time ago.

"Come on!" she said. "This is your thing, isn't it? Let's return to nature!"

She let the waves slam into her. I had never seen anyone this aggressively uninhibited. It was only the second day. Where would things go?

"I'm tempted to get naked myself and show her what she's up against," Kimberly said.

"I know you're not serious," I said. "Therefore, I'm going to the deck for a nap. That's enough of an eyeful for me today."

"I'll be up in a few," Kimberly said.

Ten minutes later, Kimberly returned, still dressed.

"What happened?" I asked.

"Nothing much. I just cleared the air with her. I told her I know what's going on and that you will make your decision."

"I told you, I have already made my decision, and I'm sticking to it," I said.

"I know," she said.

"There's something odd in your voice."

"Odd? How so?"

"I don't think you believe me."

"I know the power of what you're up against," she said. "Be ready for anything."

"Okay, then."

"I'm going to get lunch ready," she said.

She went inside. I was alone for a few more minutes when Liliana came up on the deck, stark naked and dripping wet, with a big smile.

"Where's she at?" she asked.

"She's getting something together for lunch," I said. "And get dressed, will you? I understand the world's gone crazy, but what you're doing isn't right."

"Fine," she said. "I left my clothes down at the beach. I'll get them in a second."

I sighed and stood up to leave. She rushed me, threw her arms around me, wrapped her leg around my leg, and tried to kiss me. I shoved her back.

"I will throw your ass out if you don't stop it," I said. "You're not just trying to steal me away from Kimberly, are you? What is going on? Speak up, or you're gone."

There was a towel hanging over a lounger. She wrapped herself in it, sat down, and began to cry.

"I came to another place before I came here," she said. "I had no way to know if it was safe or not. It was one of those little clusters of houses along the shore. I'm sure it was a nice place in the old days.

"There was a group of people there. Suburban types. They seemed so normal. I was so relieved. They took me in, fed me, and gave me a room in one of the better houses. I should've been suspicious.

"It was a week gone by when I realized I wasn't there because of their kindness. I was a slave."

"A warlord," I said.

"Yes," she said, still crying. "I ended up in the harem of a guy they called Solomon."

I sat up at the mention of that name. The same guy threatened to take Kimberly and sent his men to do it. He hadn't come himself. He was still out there, somewhere, doing his thing to young ladies like Liliana. My opinion of her softened a bit.

"Well, you're safe here," I said. "He sent some of his goons here to try to take Kimberly. Didn't go well for them."

"Really?" She said. "My gosh, you guys must be really badass!"

"Just bad enough, I guess," I said. "But you have got to cool it with this seduction behavior. You don't have to have sex with me to stay here. Kimberly is my wife. You can be our guest if you calm down."

"Okay, I'm sorry."

The conversation died for a minute. I wondered where to direct the conversation next. I wished Kimberly would return. Liliana sat quietly, staring off toward the sea, with the world's weight on her face.

"What are you not telling me, Liliana?" I asked.

"I haven't told you about my sister," she said. "Angie."

"Where is she? Is she okay?"

She teared up again, crying harder this time. "Solomon has her, too."

I tensed up, really wishing Solomon's neck was in my hands at that moment.

"She's ten years old," Liliana said.

I had nothing to say. If Solomon had a compound, it would be full of armed men and women. Trying to launch a rescue mission would be suicide. I couldn't figure out how to put this to Liliana.

"There's only one way I can make Angie safe," Liliana said.

I didn't like the sound of that at all. "How's that?"

"She hasn't been spoiled yet. None of the men have been allowed to touch her. As long as I do as Solomon wants, he'll let us both go."

My temper grew hot, but I wanted to stay calm and avoid scaring her into silence.

"What does Solomon want?"

Liliana stopped crying and looked straight at me with an expression of ice. "He wants Kimberly."

I glared at her. "What about me? What were you to do about me?"

"Find a way to kill you."

"Well, that's gratitude for you."

"What choice did I have? If I don't help Solomon get Kimberly, he told me he will pass Angie around to his men."

Solomon did have a fondness for passing women around.

Liliana looked to the house to make sure Kimberly wasn't approaching. She leaned in and spoke low and urgently.

"Listen, I can't do that," she said. "I don't want to kill you. You're a much better man than him. I want to be with you. I want to go with you. Come with me, and we can sneak in there and save Angie. I know where she stays. I know all those houses up and down. We can do it!"

"Did you hear what I said?" I asked. "Kimberly is my wife."

"Oh, come on. You can't tell me you love that old lady. She was your only option until now, that's all. She's still halfway decent-looking, and she's got a big chest. It's a great deal! We'll get each other, and my sister and I are free of Solomon. Colby, if you run away with me, I swear to God you will never regret it for a second."

I had to process what she was saying, not because I considered her offer but because none made a damn bit of sense. Can I chalk this up to the madness of the new world?

"Please come with me, help me," she said. "It's the only way to help Amy."

She realized her mistake. She sighed and rolled her eyes.

"I thought you said her name was Angie," I said.

She jumped to her feet and ran to a planter near the edge of the deck. I stood, wondering what on earth she was doing. She reached into the planter and pulled out a revolver. She aimed it at my heart. The gun wasn't one of ours.

"Where did you get that?" I asked.

"Solomon gave it to me. There's a hidden pocket at the bottom of my bag. I had it in there. Sorry. I snuck it out last night when we came outside and dropped it in the planter. In case I needed it for something like this."

Now, I hoped Kimberly would stay inside. Liliana would shoot her immediately.

"I was sent here to kill you so Solomon could have Kimberly."

"But what about you? You don't have a sister. What is your stake in all of this?"

"I'm not some whore in a harem," she said, spitting the words. "I am his number one. I'm the Sheba. I have riches and power."

"But ... ?"

"But I want out. I'm bored with it, and I'm scared all the time. It's getting weird over there. There's no security in it. I want to be free, even if it means eating rabbits and building shelters from fallen trees in the woods. You're the first person I met that I could have that kind of life with.

"I don't care about that old lady. We need to make hard choices. You can't start over with her. She can't give you children with that dusty womb of hers. When you're her age, she'll be what, eighty? Ninety? She gets to spend her golden years banging a football player young enough to be her son. What do you get?"

She shifted her posture, and the towel dropped to her feet.

"Look at me. Look at you. Just imagine the times we would have together. Let's go."

"She is my wife. We love each other and chose each other. You understand? You're not good enough for me. Now get dressed. I'm tired of looking at you."

"Suit yourself. I'll just kill you, deliver Kimberly, and stay with Solomon."

I thought that was the end. There was no hesitation in her eyes. The only card I had to play was to fake my agreement to run off with her. Like the horrible poker player I am, I tossed my ace in the trash.

I wondered how fast I would die. Would I hear the gunshot?

Before I got my answer, the patio door slid open.

Kimberly stood on the deck, aiming her AR-15 at Liliana.

"I knew it," Kimberly said. "Anyone bringing out this much heavy artillery so soon isn't looking for love."

THE DARK PLACE

"You can't win," Liliana said. "Solomon is untouchable. He's partners with the aliens. They have a deal. As long as he takes people to the military for the aliens, they let him keep some for himself. He'll never quit."

"Liliana," Kimberly said as gently as she could. "Lower your gun nice and easy."

Liliana didn't move.

"If you shoot him, you're dead for sure," Kimberly said. "You hate me too much to let me shoot you."

Exhausted, Liliana lowered her gun.

"Now drop it," I said.

The gun clattered to the deck when she dropped it. I picked it up and set it on the table, out of reach.

"You can't win," she said again dumbly. "All we can do is surrender and hope he shows mercy."

Kimberly tossed one of my T-shirts at her.

"Put this on," she said.

Liliana put on the shirt. I pulled my revolver out of the waistband of my shorts and told Liliana to sit down. She sank into a lounger. I told

Kimberly to get Liliana's bag. Moments later, Kimberly returned with it.

"Her bag has a hidden pocket," I said. "Can you find it?"

It took Kimberly less than a minute to find a small two-way radio.

I turned to Liliana. "So, what was Solomon's plan?"

Liliana said nothing. I turned to Kimberly, giving her a look that told her to play along.

"Darling, I think you're going to have to do something unpleasant again," I said.

Kimberly picked right up on it. "Should I use the big knife again?"

"Is it washed off and clean?"

"Yes, sharpened up, too."

"Very well. The big knife will do."

Kimberly turned to go back into the house. She gave me a look as if to warn me that I would have to find a way to deal with Liliana if she called my bluff.

"Now, Liliana," I said. "Tell me what you had arranged with Solomon. If you lie to me, I will remove your skin with my big knife."

Liliana sat on the lounger for a few seconds, thinking about what I told her. She looked tired, defeated.

"What's it matter now?" she asked. "Solomon wants Kimberly lying on the beach tied up and you lying beside her. Dead."

"You're supposed to radio him when you have it all arranged?"

"Yes," she said quietly.

"He's coming by boat if he wants us on the beach."

"Yeah, by boat."

"Where is his compound? "

"North of here. I don't know how far."

"How long will it take them to get down here?"

"About a half-hour, usually."

I thought about all of that and made a decision.

"Okay, Liliana, here's how this is going to work. You'll radio Solomon and tell him I'm dead, and we are laying out on the beach just as he wants. You better sell, or I'm using the knife."

I gave her the radio and told her to buck up and sound happy.

She radioed Solomon. He answered right away. She told him things were ready, just as instructed. He asked how she had done it. She told him she had shot me and overpowered Kimberly. He asked if she had approached me in the nude. She said yes, she had. He laughed, saying that approach worked every time. He told her he would arrive in about an hour and signed off.

"Solomon's gonna do worse than skin me alive," she said.

"Hey," I said. "Have faith. We might end this."

"That's right," Kimberly said. "Then we'll figure out what to do with you."

"Okay, Liliana. I have to tie you up until this is over," I said. "Inside."

Liliana's lethargy had lulled me into a false sense of security. It happened sometimes. No one can be at level-ten alert every waking second. She lunged for the pistol on the table. She raised her gun, and I raised mine. I realized at the last second that she aimed not at me but her own head. Kimberly reacted as well. Three bullets went into Liliana at the same time. She was dead by the time she fell to the deck.

Kimberly and I stood there in shock. Kimberly was distraught.

"Things were so peaceful," Kimberly said, sounding exhausted.

I went to her, hugged her, and rubbed her back. "We're not in control of events now. We'll have to ride this out best we can."

"You have a plan for this, I take it?" she asked.

"You bet. We'll go back to those peaceful times when this is over."

"I will not let them take me alive, remember? I will not become Liliana."

"I know. If we do this right, we won't have to worry about him anymore," I said. "Take Liliana's revolver. That way, if things go sideways, you can end it."

"I would rather this all worked," she said. "So, let's make sure we do this right, okay?"

Solomon had told Liliana he would be an hour in coming, but he could show up at any time. We made our preparations right away. We made sure our weapons were loaded and ready to go. I removed the bloodied shirt from Liliana's body and put it on. It was wet and sticky and thoroughly unpleasant, but it was so soaked with blood I figured it would give the impression we wanted.

We walked down to the gate and looked out at the sea, making sure he wasn't already on his way. There was no sign of them, so we hurried to the water line. I wrapped a short piece of rope around her wrists and ankles. They were untied so she could move her hands and feet when the time came. Her revolver was stuffed down the back of her shorts and Liliana's under her stomach.

I positioned myself on my back, feet toward the water, arms splayed out above my head—the sort of position Liliana would have left me in had she dragged me there by my feet. A revolver was under each hand.

Since I was playing dead, it was up to Kimberly to decide when to start the attack. When she fired, I would rise from the dead.

Our timing was fortunate. Kimberly saw the small motorboat approaching before I heard it.

"They're coming," she said. "There's three of them."

She spoke softly, barely moving her lips so they couldn't see her speak.

"Is Solomon with them?" I asked, also mumbling.

"Short, dark, intense-looking guy?"

I was elated. "That's him."

The sound of the motorboat grew louder.

"Okay, hush. They're almost here."

"No matter what, I love you," I whispered.

"Hush!"

The boat engine grew louder and went silent. They had arrived. They stopped far enough out to preserve the propellers. I heard a splash as they dropped anchor. Then I heard three men jumping into the water and walking toward shore. Then, it was silent for an uncomfortable few seconds. I knew he was studying me, watching if I was breathing. I held my breath, hoping I could hold it long enough.

"Where's Liliana?" Solomon asked.

I remembered his voice.

"She's inside," Kimberly said. "Bagging up all our food and booze."

"That's our girl," he said. "How are you, darling? I've been looking forward to getting to know you better. You'll be happy to know I've cleared my schedule, and we'll have all night to—"

We never found out what he planned to do. Kimberly had sprung from her false bindings and shot Solomon in his left thigh. I took a gun in each hand and sat up. They looked at me in shock.

When I brought my pistols to bear, Kimberly had shot the man to Solomons's left. The third man managed to get off a shot before I unloaded on him with both barrels. His round thudded into the sand. Like most real gunfights, it ended quickly.

I got to my feet and shot each henchman in the head and heart. I pulled Solomon to his feet. He growled in pain and let his body slack, refusing to cooperate.

"Have it your way, Your Majesty," I said.

I tossed him over my shoulder and carried them toward the pier. He tried to claw at me. I punched his wound. He behaved after that. Kimberly jogged along behind us.

"Where are you taking him?" She asked.

"I've had something special waiting for him," I said.

"Don't lose control!" she said.

She didn't want a repeat of how I'd treated Solomon's goons.

"Don't worry."

I carried him to the end of the pier. A rope and a cinder block sat there. I had run them out earlier, just in case I had this opportunity. His head faced my back. He didn't see them until I dropped him on the wood. When he saw what I had planned, he struggled to crawl away. I could've punched his wound again but watching him try to get away was more fun. All my fury at everything that had happened now had a face to focus on.

"You're not much of a man, are you?" I asked him. "Nothing without your men. You're good at manipulating other people to do your dirty work. Now me, I do my own dirty work."

One end of the rope was already tied to the cinder block. I tied the other end around his neck.

"I am protected!" he screamed. "You can't touch me! If you kill me, they will come looking for me! They will know it was you! They marked me! I was chosen! Are you?"

I stopped tying his neck for a moment. "What do you mean you're marked? Marked how?"

He bowed his head forward and pointed at a leech-looking thing stuck to the back of his neck.

"There," he said. "They gave me this. A long time ago. I told you this wasn't something that just happened out of the blue a couple of months ago."

The odd slimy thing was about 4 inches long and an inch wide. I grabbed it and pulled. Solomon screamed like I'd set him on fire. It was stuck in him. I saw tentacles running out of the thing and into his body through his neck. I pulled harder, and it stretched out a little more but wouldn't come out. I didn't feel like listening to Solomon scream anymore, even though it was satisfying.

"What is that?" Kimberly asked.

"Rulers of earth," Solomon said, gasping.

"I don't care about your aliens, Solomon," I said.

I made sure the rope was tight around his neck. I lifted him to his feet.

"You think since everything is lawless, you can hurt people as much as you want," I said. "But there's a higher law. And I'm holding you to account. Any last words?"

Of course, the fool would have some last words. I shoved him into the water before he could say anything else. He came to the surface, treading water and grimacing in pain as he kicked his wounded leg underwater. He looked up at the cinder block.

"I'm looking at a dead man," he said, still defiant.

I held the cinder block in front of me.

"Drowning is a horrible way to die, Solomon."

I tossed the cinder block into the water. He watched, wide-eyed, as the rope strung out into the water behind it. The last of the rope flew off the deck and yanked his neck hard. He gritted his teeth and fought against it. It was the first sign of real strength I had seen from him yet. When he tired out, the cinder block pulled so hard he flipped upside down. His boots burst through the surface, kicking and splashing as they sank again.

I stared at the water where he had been. Kimberly joined me.

We stayed on the pier for a half hour, waiting to see if Solomon had somehow escaped the rope. There was no sign of them. The beach was wide open, nowhere for him to sneak out of the water without being seen. We looked at each other with weary relief. The setting sun turned the sky orange.

"What will become of us if we have to keep doing this?" she asked. "How many people have we killed?"

"People?"

"You know what I mean," she said. "I know we have to go to dark places to survive. I'm worried we won't be able to come back from the dark someday."

I looked at her. Seeing the beauty and calm in her face eased the tension in mine.

"As long as we have each other, we'll find our way back," I said.

I took off Liliana's shirt.

"I've never needed a shower so badly," I said.

"Me, too. Although there's no hot water."

"Let's do it anyway," I said. "I need to purge all of this. It's ugly."

"Come on," she said, pulling me away. "Let's take a cold shower, and then I'll warm you up."

After a quick cold shower and a long, hot night in the tower, we had plenty to talk about. We agreed that Liliana had told us the truth, at least the part about people being taken from the shelters to who-knows-where. There was no denying the alien thing stuck in Solomon's neck.

"I'd say all of this is crazy," Kimberly said. "But what was crazy in the old world makes perfect sense now."

"Hell, the new world wasn't even sorted yet," I said. "Who knows just how normal crazy will get."

"Maybe there are enough people like us to build something better, so generations coming up to live in peace."

"I think that's exactly what will happen," I said.

We fell asleep together and dreamed of that world.

Road Trip

I remember being terrified in the night as a child. I'd wake up disoriented, coming out of a bad dream, unsure of what was real and what wasn't in those first few seconds. I would seek out Mom or Dad. They'd calm me down, assuring me it wasn't real, just a bad dream.

Then there are the times when you feel that numbing sense of terror because danger is really upon you.

I awoke to Kimberly clutching my arm. Her fingernails dug into my skin. I sat up, shaking myself awake, getting my bearings, and trying to remember the time and place I occupied in the real world.

Some disgusting creature lay upon her. It was about four feet long. Its skin, for lack of a better word, was slimy and pale gray. It had six spindly legs—three on each side—emerging from a slug-like body. Each leg was tipped with clawed fingers that looked razor-sharp. There were two joints in each leg. A scorpion-like tail curled up from its bottom, ending in a sharp point. Its round head resembled that of a mosquito, with bulbous black eyes and a foot-long, needle-like beak, the issue of which was stuck into Kimberly's inner thigh. Its body pulsated. It was feeding.

Kimberly was taught and frozen, every muscle flexed. Her face stretched tight in a grimace of pain and terror. Her eyes rolled sideways to look at me, pleading. It took less than one second of mental math to realize our alien friends found a way to pay a visit.

I acted without thinking, trusting instinct to guide me. If it took notice of me, it didn't react. I rolled off the bed and ran to her side. I put my hands around the thing's gooey neck and pulled its probe out of her thigh. Its legs thrashed, giving her dozens of cuts along her naked body before I pulled it away.

The creature made a soft, urgent, clicking sound. It hammered the pointed tip of its tail into my upper arm two times before I could grab it and hold it still. I now had the thing by the neck and the tail. I held its back to me and away from the bed. The thrashing claws swiped at the air for now.

Kimberly's body relaxed. Something about that stinger being in the skin had caused the paralysis. She groaned in pain and caught her breath. She sat up, clumsy and groggy, and reached for the revolver on her nightstand.

"No!" I said. "Don't shoot!"

She didn't have a good shot, and I couldn't hold thing still. It was hard to control, but thankfully, not very strong. Its bladed claws, ferocity, and stinger were its means of attack and defense. My upper arm throbbed in pain like acid had been poured into the hole. I worried the stinger was venomous. But I felt no ill effects other than the feeling of my arm on fire.

"Should I get a knife?" she asked.

'Still too dangerous!"

Weapons in close quarters with this writhing monster was too risky. I had to find a way to kill it with my bare hands. I wanted it outside, out of the house, immediately.

I carried it downstairs through the living room. I told Kimberly to remove the barricade to the patio door. It struggled like crazy. It would wear me out if I didn't deal with it soon, especially with my wounded arm.

She pulled the patio door aside. As I ran out to the deck, it struck at me. Its tail grazed my thigh. It was not a nasty wound, but it hurt like hell. I lost my temper. I lifted the thing and brought it down hard on the deck. It clickety-clacked at me, but it didn't appear to be stunned. My rage brought clarity.

"Did you kill my parents? Huh?" I asked it. "Did you kill my sisters, you piece of shit?"

I slammed it five more times. It was stunned but kept thrashing. I couldn't keep up that level of effort much longer. By now, the thing was working its way around to face me. I couldn't stop it. Its flesh was too slick and slimy. Its claws cut me dozens of times as its legs whipped about. Anytime it might strike an artery.

"Open the back gate!" I shouted.

Kimberly ran inside for the keys and rushed ahead of me to unlock the gate. She shoved it open as I ran through.

"What are you going to do?" she asked.

"See if he can swim," I said. "And hope the damn things aren't amphibious."

I ran into the sea. The alien struggled harder when the cold water touched it. It hated being wet. Good. I waded into the waves until the water danced at my waist. I held the thing under. By moonlight, I saw bubbles rising to the surface. It breathed oxygen somehow. I could add that to our list of scientific discoveries that evening.

Finally, the tension in the thing slackened in my hands. And soon after that, it was utterly still. I held it under for another five minutes to be sure. It was dead.

I returned the thing to the beach and plopped it on the sand. Kimberly and I were each covered in blood from numerous cuts. Kimberly was barely able to stand up. She dropped to her butt on the sand and rested her hands on her knees.

"Are you okay?" I asked.

She checked herself for cuts and examined the puncture wound in her thigh.

"Damn thing was drinking my blood," she said. "Ow, this hurts."

"It's your fault for being such a good vintage."

"Feels like the worst muscle pull in the world," she groaned. "Oh, my God."

"We should get the first aid kit," I said.

"How about you? Are you okay?" she asked. "You look like Carrie on prom night."

"Who?"

"Never mind."

I checked myself. I was as bloody as Kimberly, but no gushing wounds.

"Superficial cuts, I guess," I said. "Thank God he missed the sensitive stuff."

Kimberly examined her chest. She had a couple of cuts there, but the worst was from the waist down.

"I don't know how he missed those things," I said.

"Shut up," she said. "We need to clean those holes in your shoulder. Good Lord, it hurts all over."

We stood silently for a moment, staring down at the thing. We caught our breath and calmed down.

"Well, I guess they aren't beautiful and benevolent," Kimberly said. "Big surprise. What do you think we should do with it?"

"You think they're good eating?"

That got the reaction I wanted.

"Let's just leave it here to rot," I said. "Maybe some wild animals will come down and acquire a taste for it. Could work in our favor."

The first aid kit was well-stocked, but it had seen some use. I'm sure it was on Dad's list to get it filled up. We worried our wounds would need treatment beyond our competence. There were no doctors to visit. We took another cold shower—under less-romantic circumstances—and washed each other's wounds. The puncture on Kimberly's thigh was hideous, but it looked clean enough.

We covered each other in antiseptic ointment, gave each other shots of antibiotics, and used up the bandages to cover the worst of it. We made a late-night search of the house to ensure we had no other visitors. The sun was up by the time we finished. We were exhausted, yet sleep eluded us.

It hurt to wear clothing, so we were back to being nudists. Neither of us looked attractive at the moment. We had to manage until the inflammation went down.

We checked the doors and windows to see how it got into the house. It didn't take long. Liliana had opened her window for air while she slept.

In the chaos that followed her, we had overlooked it. I kicked myself for my carelessness, although I was relieved that the answer was simple.

Solomon had not been lying about the aliens. He had promised me they would come, and they had. Were they looking for him? Did they know I had killed him and therefore sought to punish me? The attack had raised more questions than it answered.

The aliens were brilliant. They had flying craft. They had flown whatever great distance they came from to get to Earth. They engineered a beam that killed according to blood type. But the thing that attacked us seemed low-level, primal. There might be a hierarchy. Drones and workers, commanders, maybe some ultimate king or queen. They were aware of us. What did that portend?

After a few days, the cuts began to scab over. We stopped taking painkillers. The muscle aches died down. Only two serious problems remained. The puncture wounds in my shoulder were still open and raw, requiring several daily cleanings. The hole in Kimberly's thigh didn't look good. Despite our efforts to keep it clean, it turned color and started to smell.

"We're going to have to go out and look for medicine," I said.

"We're out of antibiotics. The antiseptic creams are all gone. All this damage from one attack? We get messed up like this again? Infection might kill us."

"We should start in the village," I said. "Hopefully, it's abandoned. There might be something that hasn't been stripped clean."

The village, as we called it, was an all-purpose convenience store that catered mainly to the isolated houses that dotted the nearby shore. There are a few cabins surrounding it and an old-fashioned gas station. You could buy anything there, even mail a letter. Roughly twenty-five people lived there. I guessed it was among the first to be hit when things went south. If we were to find medical supplies of any kind, that would be the logical place to look. The roads were so isolated and out of the way I thought we could get there and back without any trouble.

Besides a lack of medicine, we had to worry about the possibility of warlords. Even a group of half-assed losers hiding out there could be a real problem.

"It's early in the day," I said. "I'll take the Navigator and drive down there, see what they got. You lock the gate behind me."

"Oh, no. I'm going with you. We're in this together."

She was right. Whatever we faced, we had to face it together. And it was dumb to even think about letting her out of my sight for one more second.

We gathered our weapons and bags of supplies and loaded the Navigator. If we had something to trade, it might keep us alive.

Unlocking that front gate took more courage than I expected. It had been a couple of months since I left the property. I pictured aliens pouncing from all sides as soon as we passed the gate. Kimberly stepped out of the truck and swept her rifle around the area while I secured the gate behind us.

It was a quiet drive to the village. We followed the winding path back to the county road and arrived without trouble. It was so uneventful there's nothing to report about it. It would've made a nice, leisurely drive through the country if it hadn't been for the tension of wondering what might leap at us.

The village lay just beyond the next hill. We would see it when we were right up upon it. We crested the hill and entered the village. I pulled up to the mini-mart, parked, and sat for a moment. We looked around, wondering what might greet us.

There were three cabins across the road. Small ones. The windows were broken, and the doors smashed open. They were empty, as far as I could tell. The gas station looked undisturbed, although it was hard to know because it was close to one hundred years old. I expected the gas pumps to be empty, but it would be worth checking.

The mini-mart looked just as it had the last time I was here. No broken windows. No vandalism that I could tell. I saw the floor littered with boxes and shelving through the glass door.

"Looks like the place has been looted," I said.

"You think they would've stolen medicine and things like that?" Kimberly asked.

"I suppose they've taken everything they could carry."

"You think it's worth a look? Lots of places for someone to hide," she said. "Or should we get out of here?"

I thought about her question as I looked around, checking every window, door, crack, corner, or tree. Any place somebody might hide.

"Well, we're here and were armed," I said. "And we need medicine. Let's go for it."

Kimberly stayed close to the front to watch the vehicle. I ran up and down the aisles, kicking things out of my way and righting shelving units to get through. It didn't take me long to find the medicine aisle. As I feared, it was picked clean. The section was smashed, and shelves and hangers lay everywhere. I dug through it carefully, hoping there would be something. The next option was to continue to less familiar territory.

I lifted a section of pegboard and knew God was watching out for us. There was a case of antiseptic ointment on the floor, under a bottom shelf. There were twelve tubes in the box. Jackpot.

There was nothing else there worth scavenging. It was best we got the hell out of there immediately. I met Kimberly at the front, waving the box of ointment in the air. We were relieved.

I was about to crawl into the Navigator when I saw Kimberly looking up the road, worried.

It was a ragged group of five—men, women, and children—standing together in the middle of the road. Like us, they were armed.

THOMAS

We faced each other for a two-hour minute. They were a rough-looking bunch: an older man in his fifties, a young fellow my age, two teenage girls, and a woman who looked fortyish. The stress and dirt of living in those times made it hard to be sure.

"Are we gonna stand like this forever?" Kimberly whispered.

"If nobody's shooting by now, nobody wants to," I said.

I carefully waved at them. "Hello there!"

The older man waved back. "Hello."

"We were just leaving," I said. "We mean no harm to anyone."

"We mean no harm either," he said. "We could use some food, though. Anything left in that store we might could use?"

"It was picked clean by the time we got in there," I said. "We just came for medicine. Didn't have much luck there, either."

They looked disappointed and uncertain what to do next.

"We have some food," Kimberly said. "It's not much, but we'd be happy to share. You folks look like you could use something to eat."

"Indeed we could," he said. "Been a couple of days."

"What do you say we lower our weapons," I said. "And let's be friendly."

He studied me for a second. It agonized him to show trust in anyone. I've never seen human beings look more exhausted. Kimberly lowered her rifle behind me and carefully slung it over her shoulder. She opened the Navigator's back door and took out a box we had filled with canned goods. She brought it to the front of the car and set it down.

The others looked at each other. They didn't speak but somehow communicated that it was in their best interests to be trusting. He lowered his weapon.

"Much obliged," he said.

After things thawed out between us, we gathered around the fire pit near the cabins. The man's name was Thomas. He was ex-military and had deserted his position at one of the military shelters. I wondered if he was the special friend Liliana had told us about. Seemed unlikely. The two teenage girls were Mallory and Aubrey. They were sisters who had lost their parents.

The man my age was Bob. I wonder if that was his real name. He never spoke, they said. They didn't know his real name or even what his voice sounded like. He was in total shock, barely holding on to his sanity. The other adult woman introduced herself as Mickey.

They were wandering survivors. They didn't explain where they hailed from or how they came together. It wasn't necessary. Everyone had the same story—loved ones lost, future in doubt.

We listened as they talked and watched them eat their first meal in days. I glanced at Kimberly, wondering what she thought. She felt my look and met my gaze. She nodded slightly.

"We have a house," I said.

After the nightmare of Liliana, we had resolved never to take in refugees again. But it felt wrong to leave these people sitting here without making the offer. Only Thomas looked dangerous. He was ex-military, trained in different ways to kill someone, and still healthy. I'd have to watch him close, just as he'd watch me. My instinct told me he wanted to survive in an honorable way.

"You could stay with us," I said.

"There's room for you," Kimberly said. "Our house is secure. We're not doing too bad there."

None of them seemed enthused by the invitation.

"That's most kind of you, folks," Thomas said. "But we've tried staying in one place. All that taught us is that there's no safe place for long. We've lost people that way. Now, we figure it's best to keep moving. As you can tell, it ain't the best existence, but we managed this way for a month."

"Where will you go?" Kimberly asked. "Is there a place you know of?"

"Resistance armies are assembling all over the country. I don't know about the rest of the world, but it's definitely happening here," Thomas said. "We've met scouts telling us there's a battalion working its way north. That's why we're working our way south. If we find them, we'll join up with them. Hopefully, they can give these youngsters home and comfort."

"How fast is this resistance army moving?" I asked.

"I don't know for sure. Last I heard, it was touch and go, but they were inching forward. For now, we have to avoid the evil that's out there. Make sure you folks stay away from these alien things at all costs."

I gestured toward the cuts on our arms. "We've encountered them already."

He looked surprised. "And you're still alive? You folks are made of sturdy stuff."

"It wasn't easy," I said. "Is there anything at all you can tell me about these things? Are they really aliens from another planet?"

"Another planet. Another dimension," he said. "I don't suppose the specifics matter. They want all the A-positive human blood they can get. They're so organized and efficient, it's hard for me to imagine they're doing this without help from the world's governments."

"How on Earth would these leaders benefit from helping them do this?" Kimberly asked.

Thomas shrugged. "Immunity, maybe. A promise to leave them and their families alone?"

"We were told that people are being herded into the shelters only to be taken away in the middle of the night," I said. "Do you know anything about this?"

"Yes, I know what's happening in the shelters," he said. "That's the reason I deserted."

"So where are they being taken?" I asked.

"Bear in mind, this is all scuttlebutt that I heard from my fellow soldiers, but these aliens have their own bases here and there," he said. "From what I've heard, these bases are in natural areas — deserts, forests, you get the idea."

"But not water," I said.

"No, not water. Maybe in the woods, hidden in the trees. Their ships are landing in these locations and taking off. The government buses are taking these people to those alien bases to turn them over."

"To milk them? You know, for their blood?" Kimberly asked.

"Milk them, yes, that's how to put it," he said.

I remembered the strange lights we had seen on the other side of Blackjack Hill. Kimberly looked at me, and I knew she remembered it, too. We'd heard the sounds of trucks or other large vehicles driving in the distance. The alien creatures had attacked us, suggesting they were close and spreading out.

"Can these things be beaten?" I asked. "I mean, I know they are made of flesh and can be destroyed. I drowned one, but it nearly bled me to death. Is there a way to overcome their numbers and their ferocity?"

"In the early days, when these things started crawling out of their ships, we got into a firefight with a hive of them," Thomas said. "There were a lot of them, but we shot them down easy enough. I don't know where they come from, but they haven't evolved armor. They're not that strong, but they're intelligent and nasty. Well, it's a lot to overcome. Another thing we learned is that each hive has its own leader."

"Does it stand out from the others?" I asked.

"Oh yes," Thomas said. "It's pale white, about 7 feet tall. Looks like a damn praying mantis. If you ever see it, you'll never forget it. If you do see it, you open up on it until it stops moving because if you do that, the rest of the hive will go into disarray. They get stupid or something, fall down on the ground, and are easy pickings."

After that, the conversation lulled into silence. I knew some alien camp was on the other side of Blackjack Hill. The aliens, the mantis, people being milked of their blood—all on the other side of the hill. Sleep would not come easy.

Kimberly nudged me and jutted her chin toward the sun. It was low. Darkness came earlier that first week of October.

"We need to head back, and Thomas," I said. "You sure you won't come with us?"

"Thank you, Son, but we'll keep heading south."

We stood, ready to go our own way.

"How would we know this resistance army from the official army if we were to encounter it?" I asked.

"They're unofficially known as the Apple Brigade," Thomas said. "If they offer you apples, or if you offer them apples, and either side accepts the Apple, that's the sign."

"Why apples?" Kimberly asked.

"It's a derivation from A-positive. A-plus. A-plusses. Apples. Corny, but it works."

We didn't have any apples. Very few people did unless they grew wild.

"Godspeed your way, my friends," Thomas said.

We gave them another box of supplies and said farewell.

The drive home was just as uneventful as the drive down.

Foreplay that night meant slathering ointment. Very sexy. Kimberly and I discussed everything we knew so far, the information we'd gathered from experience and Thomas. We were convinced of some "blood farm" on the other side of the distant Blackjack Hill.

"You know that hill is sacred to the Native Americans, right?" Kimberly asked.

"I didn't know that."

"Thomas said these things had an affinity for natural locations. Wouldn't surprise me to learn that these places had a pattern, maybe along some natural energy grid."

"I wonder how many aliens are clustered around these places."

She sat up and rested on her elbow, glaring at me. "You better not be thinking what I think you're thinking."

I shrugged. "If we're in a position to help, aren't we obligated to do so?"

She flopped back down onto the mattress.

"Events are totally out of our control now," she said. "We managed to find some happiness. But it wasn't going to last, was it? Walls are pressing in on us, forcing us to enter the danger zone and face death."

"I've been trying to ignore that possibility. You're right, though. The world's getting smaller. We need to act. We might die if we do, but if we don't, we'll die inside for sure."

"Yeah, yeah, I know," she said. "There's no avoiding it. I just need to express my fear of it, that's all."

"Whatever happens, at least we'll be together," I said.

"Until we sleep?" she asked.

"Until we sleep."

She turned to look at me. "Make love to me. Make love to me like you won't get another chance."

Serenaded by crashing waves, we lost ourselves in each other once again and found peace.

I knew Blackjack Hill. I had hiked it dozens of times since childhood. On the other side of the hill was the clearing we had encountered on the day Kimberly and I had taken the kids out for a hike—the old pirate fortress. Thinking back on the strange lights ascending and descending from the trees, it made sense that might be where their base was. If that was the case, things were slightly less awful than they seemed. Sneaking in for a peek and back out shouldn't be a problem if we were quiet and careful.

"What about armor?" Kimberly asked.

"Finally, something my dad didn't think about," I said.

"There's gotta be something we could use," she said. "What about baking sheets?"

They wouldn't stay tucked in our clothes.

"There's lumber in the garage," I said. "I could cut it down and make a shield."

"Could we carry a shield and a rifle at the same time?"

"Probably not," I said. "I'm sorry. I'm out of my depth here. I can't help thinking this will leave us horribly injured instead of dead."

"Dying would be better. I agree."

"If they're gonna get me, I want them to get me. I don't want to be maimed and at their mercy."

"Shooting and running," she said. "That's our best chance."

"And staying hidden until we can't," I said. "I don't know what their vision is like. No way to tell how light affects their sight."

"When do you think we should go?"

"Let's just stick to midnight. It's a good time to sneak around."

All we wanted was to have a look, but there was a good chance we would both be killed. I hoped it would be fast when it came and that neither of us would have to watch the other suffer. We also risked only one of us coming back alive. I couldn't decide which scenario was worse—me surviving or her.

With that in mind, we decided to have a lovely evening together, in case it was our last. Until we heard the rumble of engines in the distance, we could only wait.

What a beautiful night it was. The breeze was gentle and cool. The waves continued their steady lullaby as they crashed against the sand, a sound I've come to love more than any other. The moon was full and bright and free of clouds. We placed lit candles along the deck. We were quiet for a while, sitting together. What exactly does a couple do on their last night in Eden?

"Dance with me," she said.

"Sure. Let me see if I can find a radio or a CD player or something."

She grabbed my hand and stopped me.

"Leave the music to me."

We held onto each other, dancing slowly while she sang for us. I could tell you the songs, but I think you already know what songs would be perfect for that moment. You go ahead and think about it. Then you'll know the feeling of that perfect night.

THE OLD PIRATE FORTRESS

A t midnight, we left the house. We each carried a rifle and pistol. We dressed in black. All we had in black was a Wildcats polo and navy khaki pants for me, and black slacks and a sleeveless black blouse for Kimberly with a low-cut frilly neck.

"We are the most ridiculous commando team ever to have existed," I said.

Her beautiful smile broke the tension interface. "Maybe, but none ever had cleavage like this."

We walked down to the back gate, passed through it, and walked along the beach toward the woods as we talked.

"If there's some kind of alien base over there, I think it's gonna be in that old pirate fortress we passed on our way back from the hike, way back when," I said. "You remember that?"

"Yes, I remember," she said. "Are we going to go up and around the long way?"

"It'll take us a few extra minutes, but it will let us come to the clearing from the blindside."

"And if there are people there?" she asked. "Will we try a rescue, get in a fight?"

"The plan is just to take a look," I said. "If we see people there, just be cool. We'll backtrack out of sight and talk about what we might do."

We entered the woods and walked up the hiking trail. The path was worn flat and easy to follow. The wind blew hard that night. Between that and the crashing waves, our movements were well hidden. It was our first time on the path since we had taken it with the kids. I'm sure it crossed Kimberly's mind, but we agreed to keep silent until we found something.

I kept a close eye on the surrounding woods. My heart raced, and my palms were slick with sweat. Every step brought the possibility of one of those hideous things charging out of the trees at us by the dozens or the hundreds. I was tense in every muscle, ready to react. The hill kept its secrets so far.

All I knew about the critters I'd learned from the one I killed. They were terrifying and gross, which gave them an advantage. A person was likely to freeze for a few seconds from shock, giving the creatures time to get the upper hand. That tail stinger was a bitch. The two holes in my shoulder still hurt like hell. Their razor claws could inflict a literal death by one thousand cuts.

Our advantages: they were petite and not strong, and their bodies were soft and fragile. The actual danger in these things was their numbers and ferocity. They could be stabbed, shot, and drowned, but you were in trouble if you let yourself get swarmed.

We reached the top of the hill, but there was no sign of critters from another world. The air was fresh and cool after crossing the tree line. We paused at the peak, feeling the moonlight on our faces. I watched the sparkling waves crash over each other and onto the sand.

"Can I confess something?" I said, keeping my voice low.

She waited.

"I'm tempted to turn away right now. Just forget all of this, pack a bag, and drive that Navigator the hell out of here," I said.

"What's stopping you?" She asked.

"Part of me doesn't want to leave here. Not just because of my family's history with it but because part of me thinks you and I could fix all this. That we can keep going with what we started. That's only part of the reason, though. The main reason is that if there are people down there, and we don't help them, I don't think we'd ever feel human again.

She hugged me. I have never needed a hug so badly in my life.

"God is on our side," she said. "I think we'll win this one. I do."

I look down at her perfect face in the moonlight. I gave her a quick kiss, and we descended to the other side of the hill toward the clearing. That part of the walk didn't take long. The path sloped toward a bend that curved around a cluster of thick trees. Just around that blind corner was the clearing. We crept to the trees and peeked into the clearing.

At first glance, the old fortress was just as we'd left it: stone ruins and a blocked cave. As our eyes adjusted to the darkness of the inner woods, we saw a split-level fence made from crudely hewn logs augmenting the stone wall. The grass in the clearing was flat everywhere. Something had been there, but it was empty and quiet.

"You think they've abandoned it?" Kimberly whispered.

I felt it before I saw it—the same oppressive sense of evil that filled our bedroom when Kimberly was attacked. I knew those things were close by. The malevolent vibe fogged the air so badly that I wondered if the aliens were demons incarnate.

I squinted my eyes shut to further adjust to the darkness. We were deep in the woods. Only isolated shafts of moonlight splintered through. I scanned the clearing carefully, moving my eyes inch by inch along the ground.

"No way is it abandoned," I whispered.

I slowly pointed them out to her, putting a finger to my lips so she wouldn't gasp or cry out.

There were about twenty of them. Not a single one moved. They either napped or hibernated. Perhaps it was necessary when they weren't attacking or feeding. They hunched on the ground, reminding me of cicadas we used to find in the trees.

I took a chance and moved closer. I wanted to see the cliffside and look at the cave. A shaft of moonlight hit the earthen wall, revealing the cave to be open, yawning into shadow. That feeling of malevolence became even more potent. I saw nothing, but I knew if one of those mantis aliens were there, that's where he slumbered.

Opposite the cave, past the clearing and beyond the stone wall, I saw a pair of tire tracks that hadn't been there before. Now, we knew this was a drop-off point. I shuddered to think what happened here when it was operating.

Kimberly poked my arm hard and fast. I looked at her, and she jutted her chin forward. I followed her gaze as best I could and saw the body—an adult woman, stiff and dead. Nearby were scattered shoes, clothing, and dark splashes that probably weren't motor oil. If there was a portal to hell, we had found it.

Kimberly looked up at me, her eyes asking what the plan was. I motioned her to hold tight and see what happened.

An iridescent glow broke through the treetops. It came from the south, coasting silently. We finally had a good look at one of the UFOs that had crisscrossed the skies for the last few months.

I worried we had waited too long to get out of there. There were so many unknowns. There was no way to know if the ship had some detection technology to sense our presence. It paused over the clearing and descended as smoothly as a helicopter, landing in the center. We ducked behind the trees to avoid being lit up by its luminosity. It hummed and vibrated for a few seconds, and then it was dark and still, sitting there in its intimidating vastness.

It went dark. We both jumped. Without its glowing lights, the thing looked like a giant pinball. We waited fifteen more agonizing minutes. We decided nothing more was likely to happen and returned home the way we had come.

Back at the house, we stripped off our fatigues and unwound on the deck. We sat in silence for a bit, each of us pondering the many questions we had.

"We should be ready to move when we hear the trucks going up there," I said. "By the time we get back to the fortress, the people will be unloaded, and that's our chance."

"Oh boy," she said. "It's getting real."

"The trees they're using for barricades aren't very thick," I said. "We have an ax in the garage. A big one. I could chop that thing open easy."

"You think that's the play?" she asked.

"I think so. We should come to the fortress from the opposite side. It's shorter," I said. "I'll cause a distraction at the top corner of the fence, by the cliff there. I'll get those things running at me. While I do that, you go to the other end and chop the wood clear. You should be able to do it quickly. Chop it down and lead the people back to the house. I'll hold them off, then follow you."

"I won't chop that wood as quick as you," she said. "You should be the one chopping the wood down. I'll have to be the distraction. Just make sure I have plenty of bullets."

She was right, of course. I hadn't suggested it her way because I didn't want her to be the distraction. If my adrenaline was pumping hard enough, and I was sure it would be, I would have that fence chopped open in about five seconds.

"What do you think happened to that dead woman up there?" she asked. "I think they drained her. Right then and there."

"Thomas said they were taking A-positive people for their blood," I said. "But they couldn't fit many people in that giant ball bearing. It's big, but not that big."

"What if it's not people they're putting in the ship?"

"I don't like where you're going with this," I said.

"One thing we know for sure is that blood is the reason they're here," she said. "Human blood."

"They're not just feeding on people with those big needle noses," I said.

"They're draining them into those ships somehow," she said. "Like an oil tanker."

"Holy cow," I said. "That has to be it, just like oil exploration. Instead of black gold, it's red gold. They kill all of humanity who doesn't have the blood they want, send their drones out to drain those still alive who have the blood they want, and fill up those ships with God knows how many gallons."

"Blood tankers," she said with a shiver. "I used to worry about nuclear war when I was a kid. The good ol' days."

"I suppose we'll find out soon enough, one way or another," I said. "It's as good a theory as any, though. Let's work from it until we know different."

Before Kimberly offered her theory, I was about to suggest a late dinner. Now, my appetite was gone.

"This is like a horror movie," she said. "And in horror movies, you have a fifty-fifty chance of getting out alive. That's why romantic comedies are better."

"If we get out of this, I promise it's only romantic comedies for the rest of my life."

She gave me that sultry look she used when it was time to turn our attention away from the unpleasant and toward the pleasant.

"And how many romantic comedies have you seen?" she asked.

"More than I care to admit."

She reached across to my chair and ran her fingertips along my thigh. I jerked away involuntarily. I'm very ticklish.

"Then you've seen enough to know what usually happens in the middle of a romantic comedy?" she asked.

"That's usually when the couple makes love for the first time," I said.

"Right answer," she said. "Only I'm very stressed. I'm in the mood for something far beyond 'making love.'"

I carried her up to the tower. The way we came together was the only way to rest our minds from what the world had become.

JAILBREAK

Distraction was a constant state of mind by then. We stayed busy. The house needed cleaning. The grounds required tending. Company might be coming if our mission succeeded. We got things ready as if we expected family for Christmas.

Staying on the move didn't erase the conclusions Kimberly and I came to the night before. The realization of what took place on Blackjack Hill was deeply disturbing. The images it brought to mind were ghastly and insistent, difficult to purge from the imagination. But there was more than that. There was a dimension to it that I hadn't thought of, probably because it was too dark a place to go.

"What are they doing with all the bodies?" I asked.

Surprised, Kimberly looked up at me as I hit her with that question as I walked into the kitchen.

"Just thinking about our conversation last night," I said. "They're draining the bodies to fill the tankers. What are they doing with the bodies?"

Kimberly leaned against the counter for support. "Oh my God. I don't know. Do I have to think about that?"

"If this is some kind of exploratory mission to find natural resources they need, then our bodies would be like industrial waste to them," I said.

"All right, stop it," she said. "Something horrible! Okay? They're disposing of them somehow, somewhere. It's beyond what any decent human being could think of."

"You're right," I said. "We just have to stop them. If we could stop them here, that would be a win. A small win, but a win."

"I think that's the best way to look at this," she said. "We could go insane trying to figure out just how very awful they are. Let's accept that they are bad and need to be stopped."

She was right. It was difficult to accept the reality of such bottomless evil. I felt as though I had done all the accepting I could do.

I went to the beach for a jog to clear my head and calm my anxiety. It didn't work. Instead of clearing my mind, I brainstormed numerous scenarios under which the aliens might be disposing of bloodless bodies. Maybe they were burning them or burying them in some giant pit. To be taken out to sea and dumped for the sharks. We had only seen one body inside the fortress. We'd seen no smoke, smelled no horrible odors, and there was no way the sheer number of people being taken to these bases were being put into those ships. They weren't big enough, and there weren't enough of them coming and going.

I wish I could tell you we discovered what happened to them, but we never did. And no official explanations were offered in the days after it was over. That meant one of two things: they honestly didn't know, or the truth was too horrible to speak aloud.

I ran past the gate when Kimberly came running out, waving her arms.

"I hear engines!" she said.

This was a break in the routine. Usually, we heard the engines at night. Now, it was midmorning. I could tell Kimberly had the same thought.

"It's broad daylight," she said. "Is now the right time? Or should we wait for them to come at night?"

"We don't know if light affects their vision," I said. "I assume we'd have an advantage at night, but who knows?"

"They don't usually come in the daytime," she said. "You think they know we snooped around?"

I was frightened. Can't lie. Day or night, there were only two choices—stay at home, knowing people were being killed, or try to help, knowing we would likely be killed ourselves.

"Let's go," I said.

We didn't bother with improvised commando clothes. We grabbed the rifles, the pistols, the big ax, and Kimberly had a butcher knife. We split the last box of ammo.

We reversed course on our way to the fortress. We ran along the outside of the fence until we came to the place we usually came out. Going this way got us there faster and allowed us to approach from behind a hill. My familiarity with the area was our only sure advantage. We didn't know if surprise was on our side. For all we knew, they had a trap ready for us.

We came over a ridge and huddled down. Soldiers shoved the last few people off a school bus. Men, women, and children screamed in terror when they realized they had been betrayed. Soldiers forced them into the makeshift corral and fastened the wooden gate. The aliens herded the people into the center of the corral. They filed in around the giant craft, which stood still and silent.

"Can't believe soldiers would do this," Kimberly hissed. "Traitors."

"Let's wait for them to leave," I said. "They'll kill us for sure."

The bus pulled away, empty. It was disappointing because I was angry enough to execute my fellow human beings at that point for daring to participate in such a thing.

"Can you estimate how many?" I asked. "Looks like fifty or so to me."

"At least," she said.

Her lips quietly counted. "Sixty, give or take."

"If they have some fight in them, they might help us."

The alien slugs surrounded the people and started separating them into groups. No time would be wasted. The large metal sphere sat quiet and ominous in the middle of everything. These people were going to be drained immediately.

"Remember the plan?" I asked.

"You go right. I go left."

"Make sure you don't shoot any kids by mistake."

"Screw you," she said. "Don't be forever chopping that fence down, Mr. Tight End."

We kissed and got to our feet.

Some of the prisoners spotted us as we rushed the fence. At first, they weren't sure what to make of us. We weren't part of the operation. We were sneaking in. They put it together fast. They shouted and pointed, desperate with hope. The aliens, likely not understanding what they said, what their body language indicated, or much caring, continued their work of preparing people for draining. Several aliens took positions along the fence to prevent people from escaping. Those aliens saw us.

Kimberly ran alongside me to my left. I pointed to where the corral fence met the cliff wall. She veered off to run to that corner of the fence as I ran to the opposite end.

Just as I reached the corner, an alien on the outer perimeter sensed my movement and turned to see what was happening. I swung my ax on the run and took its head off. It didn't take much of a swing. They were fragile behind their frightening appearance and energy. Red blood mixed with jade-colored muck splattered out from its stump.

I reached the corner and chopped at the rail logs. One swing for each of the two logs. I grinned at Kimberly. Sadly, she didn't see it.

Screams erupted from the crowd. The aliens had started stabbing them with their needle-like snouts.

Shots rang out as Kimberly opened fire on a pair of aliens near the metal sphere. They fell to the ground, convulsing momentarily, then were still.

Several prisoners caught on that a rescue of some sort was underway. A few of them got with the program and started fighting against the aliens, punching, kicking, and trying to run away. Kimberly carefully picked her shots and did a great job taking out one alien after another, avoiding prisoners. We hoped the creatures would dumbly rush toward the source of the attack rather than flee it. We were right. Those things mindlessly ran toward her, away from the people.

I waved and shouted at everyone to run through the opening I had created in the corral. There were no old people in this group. Everyone there had working legs capable of jogging away from the base. That would make our job easier.

A tall man ran by. I held out the ax.

"Help us out, will you?" I asked.

He hesitated, then took the ax. An alien came through the fence's opening, upright, clattering along on his back four legs, waving his top two legs at us. My new ally swung his ax like a champ and buried it in the thing's thorax. It fell to the ground. With a couple more blows, it was dead. The man stood up and looked back at me with a big smile.

"That felt good!" he said.

I gave him a thumbs up. "Keep choppin'!"

Our approach confused the aliens. They were attacked from one side, and their quarry escaped from the other side. All prisoners were clear of the fence and running toward the hill. I was elated. If we could get everybody over to the other side, I would feel good about our chances of returning to the house. We could run faster than those things could scurry.

I shouted at Kimberly to retreat. She nodded and turned to run. I ran backward a few steps, getting ready to turn and run, when something came out of the cave. It was tall, sickly, pale, and looked like a giant praying mantis. In one of its spindly hands, it held some object. It looked like a torch if the handle were a bone. A smooth metal sphere tipped the handle where the torch flame would be.

The mantis had slipped my mind in the chaos. Now I had a terrible feeling about that object in its hand. I implored everyone to run as fast as they could. I ran backward and sideways, trying to escape and keep an eye on the mantis.

It stepped forward slowly, step by lazy step, like one of those movie killers who knows he can walk faster than you can run. He aimed the device at us. Kimberly and roughly a third of our group were safely over the hill. The sphere on the device glowed red. I screamed for everyone to hurry, although everyone ran as fast as they could.

When I heard a child scream, I unslung my rifle to fire at the mantis. To my right, an alien had caught a young girl. Its needle stabbed into her arm. I came close enough for a safe shot and killed the thing. I got the girl to her feet and carried her away.

The alien slugs swarmed at us. A shot at the mantis would have to wait. I ran over the crest of the hill and down a couple of yards. I released the girl and was about to return for the others.

A terrible and familiar vibrating sound and feel came from the fortress. Mass screams tore at our ears from the other side of the hill. People cried out, and their voices quickly died away.

As if they had suddenly fallen asleep.

The nightmare had gone from bad to worse. There was no way to know if this weapon had been hidden or was a recent invention. The aliens now had a new—and hand-held—vibrating beam that would kill even those of us with A-positive blood. Anybody who had yet to come over the hill was never coming over.

Everyone knew what had happened and what it meant. Survivors ran in all directions, not knowing which path was safe. People whose friends and loved ones hadn't made it over shouted for help and started to run back.

I ran to the front of the group and shouted for everyone to follow me. Kimberly fell in with the group and helped me guide them. She watched me, curious about what had made me panic. It took all my strength not to sprint ahead as fast as I could to escape, not knowing how many of those weapons they had.

A few people ran back to help those left behind. Noble, but suicide. Aliens swarmed over the hill and overwhelmed them.

With the aliens busy, we led everybody out of the forest, around the fence, to the beach, and through the back gate. I grinned like a madman as everyone safely came through the fence. By God, we had done it. I told everybody to go up onto the deck and wait. I held Kimberly back. We aimed our rifles at the trailhead and waited. No aliens came.

"What the hell is going on?" she asked. "This is only like one-third of the people who were there. What happened to the rest? Did they get recaptured?"

"Did you see the thing? That praying mantis alien?" I asked. "He's got a new weapon."

"What kind of weapon?"

"Something that puts us to sleep, too," I said.

She was too shocked to respond. It was horrible news.

"Let's keep watch for a second. If that thing comes down, we have to take it out quickly, or we're all toast."

For a tense five minutes, we waited. Judging by the speed we observed, they would have appeared by then if those things were chasing us. We lowered our rifles and took a breath.

Kimberly started to laugh. I looked at her like she was crazy.

"What?" she asked. "We won! Smile, dammit, we got a win!"

I didn't rain on the parade and talk about how plenty of aliens were still alive, that they now had a beam that could kill us all, that one-third of our people hadn't made it. She knew all of that.

We had struck a hard blow. If it could be done once, it could be done again and again and again until they were all dead.

FLEEING

Kimberly and I joined the survivors on the deck after we secured the gate. There was no celebratory mood when we met them. No happiness at all. Instead of thank yous, we were swamped with dozens of questions. It seems everyone had left a loved one behind at the alien fortress. Everyone knew how they had died. The shock was understandable. The one bright ray of hope we clung to was that the beam could not hurt us. It gave us hope through all we endured. If we survived, we might see order restored and take a chance at life again. Now that hope was gone. Now, the aliens had a special beam for us, too.

There were no answers. Kimberly and I kept silent as everyone vented their frustrations and fears. After a few minutes, I grew irritated and called for silence. They ignored me. I thought about firing a few shots into the air.

A man and a woman joined us. They introduced themselves as Jeff and Monica Kipler. They waved their arms and shouted for silence. Since they had been with this group since the shelter and on the bus ride together, the others listened to them and calmed to silence.

"Please, friends," Jeff said. "We owe these two our lives. The least we can do is say 'thank you' and let them talk."

He turned to me and smiled as if he'd just introduced me at a Rotary Club meeting. I hadn't prepared a speech.

"Welcome, everyone," I said. "You're all safe for now. We're fenced in, and the house is sealed up. We have some food and water to share. We even have a working shower, if you don't mind it being cold. It ain't fancy here, but please, let's settle down and eat and drink first. Then we can talk things over. Okay?"

Kimberly and I caught our breath as everyone sat down and talked. I got a read on the interpersonal dynamics at play. People consoled each other. Everyone had lost someone.

Jeff and Monica sat at a table with two young girls. They appeared to be the only ones with their family still intact. I nudged Kimberly, nodded at the four of them, and suggested we speak with them.

We sat down at their table. They smiled at us in a way that was not natural.

"No need to be nervous," I said. "We're the good guys. I promise we'll do what we can to take care of you."

Kimberly lowered her voice. "Are these your daughters?"

One couldn't make any assumptions. Some families did survive, but sometimes, men and women paired up and "adopted" children whose parents were gone and needed protection.

Monica smiled as if she were glad to share a secret. "Yes. This is Angie and Britney."

"You're kidding!" Kimberly said. "That's amazing. An entire family with the same blood type?"

Jeff looked around, cautiously. "We prefer that information didn't get around. People are strange these days. Maybe you've noticed. You don't know what people might do with that information, especially these aliens."

"Our lips are sealed," I said.

"Well, I think we better get everybody something to eat," Kimberly said. "Jeff, would you give me a hand?"

Jeff readily agreed to help. He stood and followed Kimberly. As they walked to the patio door, Kimberly paused to ask another man to help her.

I had already spotted him before she spoke to him. He'd been talking to a girl of about eight years old. He was speaking to her in a severe manner. She looked uncomfortable. Maybe I shouldn't have thought it strange in the surreal vibe that blanketed the world. But something about it set off an inner alarm.

The man hesitated when Kimberly asked for his help. He glanced at the girl, then back to Kimberly, and nodded his agreement. He gave the young girl a quick glare and left. I would've joined them if Jeff hadn't been with Kimberly.

I felt compelled to speak with the girl. I rushed over to have a quick chat before they got back.

"How are you doing?" I asked.

She smiled stiffly and shrugged. She'd probably been told not to speak to anyone.

I had no experience in handling this sort of thing. I kept it as simple as possible.

"Let me ask you a question," I said. "You don't have to say anything. I'll make it a yes or no question. You just shake your head or nod your head to answer. That way, you're not talking to a stranger? Right?"

She smiled at that loophole.

"Is that man your daddy?"

She shook her head no. I felt a chill.

"Is he your uncle or some kind of relative?"

Another shake of the head. Neither was he any family friend, nor had she seen him before.

"You see how big and strong I am?" I asked.

She smiled and nodded as if she knew where I was going.

"If I tell you I'm not afraid of that man, and I can make sure he never bothers you again, would you believe me?"

She nodded.

"Do you want me to fix it so that man will leave you alone?"

Another nod.

"Can you tell me a secret that only your real daddy would know?" I asked.

She studied me momentarily, then said, "My favorite singer is Jim Croce."

I only knew of Jim Croce because he was a favorite of Dad's. It seemed like an unusual choice for a young girl, but I suppose her daddy had also passed along his music to her.

"I like him, too," I said. "And by the way, my name is Colby."

"I'm Joni."

"I'll tell you what, Joni. You just sit here and act like everything's the same. You leave everything to me, okay?"

This time, she nodded with a grin.

"I promise you things will be okay."

The man returned with Kimberly and Jeff, carrying bags and boxes of our dwindling food supplies. He looked to be in his forties. I approached him and offered my hand before he could look for the girl.

"Colby Swanson."

Like most people, he was taken aback by someone younger being aggressively friendly. He warily shook my hand.

"Teague."

"Teague, would you mind coming with me?" I asked. "There's something I need the men here to know."

He hesitated, but the lure of men-only secrets was too strong. He likely saw an advantage in it. He agreed. I led him to the end of the pier.

"Where are we going? What's this all about?" He asked.

He was agitated and didn't like the idea of some teenager asserting authority over him. That was fine.

"How's Joni getting along with all of this?" I asked.

That startled him. He quickly recovered and acted like things were normal. It was too late. He was caught, and he knew it.

"You only recently met this girl, isn't that right?" I asked.

He narrowed his eyes, put his hands on his hips, and looked up at me.

"Young man, have you been talking to my daughter?" he asked.

"Can it with the 'young man' crap. Are you targeting this little girl for something unnatural?"

He shifted his stance, clenched his fists, and otherwise gave every indication that he was ready to fight.

"Now listen here," he said. "You stay away from her."

"Who's her favorite singer?" I asked.

"We're done here."

He turned to leave. I grabbed his shirt and held him in place.

"Favorite singer," I said.

He looked down at my fist holding a wad of his shirt. He brought his eyes back up to mine and realized our conflict was not about his superior age but my superior size. His demeanor changed. Now, he played the poor soul who was being misunderstood.

"I don't know what she listens to," he said, trying to think of who the youngsters were listening to on the radio in the regular days. "Taylor Swift."

Have you ever given anybody a grin of pure violent fury? I did my best in that moment.

"Teague, don't let me see you within arm's reach of that girl again."

"What the hell is this? Big man with the gun, taking over people's houses? Giving orders?"

"It's my house," I said. "My great-grandfather built it when Teddy Roosevelt was president. So when you're on my property, you behave, or you'll be thrown off my property."

I'd love to tell you I was coming up with all this stern talk on my own. The truth is, I was repeating things I had heard my dad say to rivals or bullies at different times throughout my childhood.

"Well, it's a new world now, Sonny," he said. "Lots of things are going to be different."

"Yeah, you're right; things are different. There are no courts. No juries. No appeals. You'll get a taste of the new rules if you don't shape up. Are you picking up what I'm throwing down?"

He didn't answer. I released him, and he walked back down the pier.

"Hey, Teague. Remember, arm's-length. Both arms. I'm talking about the length of my arms, not yours."

I spread my arms out wide.

"From the tip of one middle finger to the other."

He left without another word.

I knew troubles with him were not over, but they were stilled long enough for me to return to continuing problems on the deck. I wasn't through the gate yet when I heard arguing. I joined the group that caught Kimberly's eye. She was shaking her head and rolling her eyes.

She met me at the edge of the deck.

"What's going on here?" I asked.

"They're debating whether everyone should stay or leave," she said.

"It's anarchy, baby," I said.

I called for the group's attention.

"Friends, this is not a prison," I said. "You can stay or go of your own free will. I don't have to tell you the risks of either option."

"How long before those things swarm us with their new beam?" someone asked.

"Minutes? Days? Weeks? I don't know," I said. "But if they do swarm, they'll get in eventually. There's too many of them."

"So, we should leave?"

"That's not for me to tell you," I said.

"How much food do you have?"

"For all of us? About two weeks. Guessing," I said.

"Is it safe out on the roads?"

"If they swarm, they'll get you in the trees for sure," I said.

"Then what's the answer?"

"Enjoy our moments while we can," Kimberly said. "Live with the fear. Fight when and how we can. If the end comes, meet it with dignity."

Finally, they were silent.

"Again, stay or leave, but remember you are guests," I said. "Let's work together to make this a place of peace. If you want out, I'll open the gate for you."

In the ruckus, I forgot to tell Kimberly about Teague and Joni. Things might've been less complicated later if I had.

Jeff joined us.

"At the shelters, we heard people whispering about a resistance army of some kind," he said. "Do you know anything about this?"

"I don't have any first-hand confirmation, but I've heard about it," I said.

"What did you hear?" he asked.

"That there's a resistance fighting its way toward us from the south. I don't know how close they are or how fast they're moving."

"The smart thing to do would be to get the hell out of here and head south, then," Teague said.

I hadn't seen him sidle up. He pretended our conversation hadn't happened.

I felt Kimberly going hot next to me.

"Again. Gate. Open. Your call," I said.

I worried we'd made a mistake rescuing this bunch. Then I remembered they were scared and scarred.

"There's something else we should discuss, " I told the group.

For the first time, everyone stopped talking.

"As you know, we lost a lot of people back there," I said. "And if you've thought about it, you've figured out what happened. I don't know if you saw that tall alien back there, the one that looked like a praying mantis. He had a weapon in his hand that shot a beam, just like the beam that killed our families. Only this beam can kill us."

That started a new round of panic and anger. I expected that, but I had to tell them.

After that information, the consensus of most of them, following another round of shouting and arguing, was to leave and head south. Jeff and Monica argued for staying, but they were the only ones. This worked to our advantage, as it reduced the numbers we had to support at the house. But I felt duty-bound to tell them what I thought was right.

"Let me remind you that we don't know where the resistance is," I said. "Or if it's real."

"There could be warlords or another alien nest somewhere along the way," Kimberly said. "We're happy to give you some food, but we can only give you a little. You don't know how long it will last."

"What about that new beam, though?" one of the women asked. "How do we know they're not coming down here right now to use it on all of us?"

"We don't know," I said. "That's why the course of action I think we should take is to go back and attack again."

I let them react to that for a second.

"The same people who told me about the resistance told me if you take out that mantis, all the other aliens connected to it will collapse," I said.

Everyone was silent, frowning at me.

"It's like they're tied together psychically. Like a hive mind or something," I said.

Teague sighed and shook his head.

"Psychic hive minds," he said, chuckling. "I see a garage there. Do you have vehicles?"

Kimberly and I looked at each other. Her look told me that if he didn't leave on his own, I should throw him out.

"We have a van," I said. "You can take it. Whatever amount of fuel it has, that's what you get."

I pointed to the picnic table.

"And you can take those two boxes of food."

Now that a vehicle with gas and a small food supply was offered, everyone but the Kipler family decided it was time to go immediately. Honestly, this group gave me heartburn. I was ready for them to leave.

We led them to Kimberly's family van. I can imagine her mixed emotions as they all piled in, taking up space in the vehicle she and her family had used for so many journeys before.

Teague was behind the wheel. I tossed him the keys.

"How do we go south?" he asked.

I gave directions to the state highway. It would give them the best chance of meeting the resistance.

All fifteen of them somehow crammed into her Odyssey van. They had to remove the seats and squeeze onto the floor. They got settled as I went to the gate and opened it.

Teague drove the van out of the property faster than he needed to. He didn't meet my eyes as he went past. I was about to close the gate when something stilled my arm. Something wasn't right.

Kimberly stood near the open garage with the Kipler family. We were the remainders. Someone was missing. I knew it. Then it hit me. Joni was in the van.

It was a stupid mistake. All I can do is plead innocence. I had no experience keeping an eye on children. If Kimberly had known, she'd have kept Joni by her side at all times.

Panicked, I looked down the roadway but couldn't see them. The road curved away quickly. The van was already going as fast as it could. I'm sure Teague felt that he had made his getaway.

I cursed myself and ran inside the house to get the keys to the Navigator. I ran out to find Kimberly standing there with her hand spread out, curious.

"What on earth is going on?" she asked.

"One of those girls is kidnapped," I said. "I'll explain when I get back."

"I'll come with you," Jeff said.

"No, stay with your family," I said.

I tore out of the driveway in the Navigator with Kimberly running to keep up. She stood by the open gate and watched me drive off.

I took the curves too fast, trying to think of how I would handle this. I came around a blind turn and saw the van had run off the road and hit a tree. I almost didn't see it.

What I did see was the van swarmed with alien creatures. All the doors and back hatch were open. None of the creatures had noticed me yet. I got out and readied my rifle.

I met the awful sight of everyone screaming as the aliens attacked. Most had two or three hideous slug things stabbing into their bodies. I had never seen a swarm this big. They cut and slashed people into submission and siphoned out their blood. The aliens had come down and hidden behind the trees. These poor people had run right into their trap. They attacked with such ferocity it felt like punishment for escaping.

I ignored people who weren't moving and did my best to shoot the aliens attacking those who still moved, although most of that was involuntary twitching by that point. People screamed, cursed, and begged for help, but there were too many, the attack too far along. It had come to this in seconds. It was a massacre, and it was too late for all of them.

I was sick, thinking I had sent Joni to her death like this.

The aliens hadn't noticed me yet, so I searched for her while I had the time. I pushed my luck. The aliens still hadn't shown any interest in me, but I knew they would look to me next when they were done with their current crop of victims.

Joni wasn't among the victims scattered along the ground. When I thought about it, I hadn't seen Teague, either. I looked around and through the trees. Teague was dragging Joni away by her hand. They weren't far, but it was dangerous to stray from the Navigator. I was not going back without her.

I fired a shot in the air. He ducked, stopped, and turned.

"Let her go," I said.

I leveled the gun at his chest. "Like you said, Teague, it's a new world. Last warning."

He released Joni's hand. I was pleased she ran to me without having to be told.

What to do with this guy?

"Joni, get in the car and close your eyes," I said.

I quickly looked around to see if the aliens were still busy. They were distracted, sniffing the air, finished with this group, and looking for more prey. It was the most dangerous moment.

Teague smirked at me. "See you later, Slick."

He turned and ran. Somehow, he had survived this attack, probably by throwing an old lady at them. I had a sinking feeling he would find the resistance, become their general, and become president. Shit floats to the top, my Dad liked to say.

Maybe I should've let him run. After talking to Joni later, I knew he hadn't messed with her in any way, but only because he didn't have a chance. His intentions were clear. No matter how good or bad of a man he was before the invasion, his path now was clear. To let him go was to condemn any number of girls to lifetime trauma.

I shot him in the ass and thigh. He screamed and collapsed to the leaves. The aliens noticed. Hundreds of bloody snouts turned in his direction. Maybe they heard the noise, or they sensed fresh blood. Either way, the entire swam rushed to him as he tried to crawl away.

I took Joni back to the house.

The Resistance

K imberly greeted me with a slap to the face when I got back. She was kind enough to wait until Jeff and Monica had taken Joni and their girls to the front. She glared at me as I explained the situation between Teague and Joni, how I hadn't had a chance to tell Kimberly about it. I told her I shot Teague and not in self-defense. She told me I did the right thing and gave me a wallop.

"We don't split up," she said, angry as I'd ever seen her. "Ever."

She stormed off. Lesson learned.

I returned to the front gate and peered through, looking for any sign of the aliens. No horde was coming down the road or around the bend, so they may have reached their quota for the moment. I knew they would be back. If we weren't on borrowed time before, we certainly were then.

I made sure the front area was secure and joined the others. Everyone stood around, quiet and puzzled. Monica and the girls held apples, looking at them as if they didn't know what they were. It made no sense for apples to be here. We had no apple trees, nor had anyone brought them.

"Where did you find them?" Kimberly asked.

"There were quite a few between the deck and the fence," Jeff said.

Kimberly and I thought of it at the same time.

"Apples!" she said, her face brightening.

"Symbol of the resistance," I said.

We explained to Jeff and Monica what Thomas told us about apples and the resistance Army. It was a bizarre connection, but they believed it and were both excited.

"Do we dare get our hopes up?" Monica asked.

"Kimberly and I will check the back gate," I said. "Maybe the rest of you should stay here. If I don't come back, or someone comes back without us, well . . ."

Kimberly gave Jeff a revolver.

"Let's hope for the best," I said.

We found four soldiers standing on the other side of the fence. They looked stressed, especially when they saw us armed. I wasn't sure how to break the ice, so I held up the apple.

"Do we have you fellas to thank for the apples?" I asked.

The oldest and biggest of the group smiled. "You folks like apples?"

"If that's code, I'm afraid I don't know the right response," I said. "But I know apples mean the resistance. Is that you?"

"That's us, all right," he said. "Sgt. Mike Wharton."

He gestured to the three younger soldiers with him.

"And these are Privates Malory, Burton, and Fletcher."

We nodded hello. Sgt. Wharton was big enough, but his three men were likewise tall and fit. If I let them in, there would be no defending against them. The sergeant sensed my hesitancy.

"Are you folks doing okay?" he asked.

"We've been doing well so far," I said. "Things are getting desperate."

If it turned out to be a mistake to let them in, I would end my life on a dumb decision and take everyone else with me.

Wharton gestured to a small military boat sitting on the beach.

"We were doing a recon patrol along the coast when a storm took us out to sea," he said. "Our boat's shot. We had to paddle in. That's how we found our way here. We need shelter, food, and some fuel if you have any to spare."

Kimberly's face was neutral. She didn't look worried, but she didn't speak up. I looked back at the four soldiers.

"I know what you're thinking, friend," Wharton said. "I wouldn't trust us either. What I can tell you is that we hate these scum creatures with a passion. They killed our families, too. Our leaders betrayed us. Believe me, we're on your side if you're good people."

I studied their faces. All of them looked tired, afraid, yet determined. I had to take the chance.

I unlocked the gate. We brought them up to meet the others. There were a few awkward moments as everybody was introduced. Sgt. Wharton did his best to put everyone at ease. Kimberly looked from him to me, trying to get my read on the situation. I nodded as if to say everything was agreeable for me so far.

We offered them food. First, Kimberly and I, and then Jeff and Monica, told the soldiers our stories. Joni shyly revealed she lost track of her parents at a shelter. We told them everything, right up to the alien massacre that had occurred out front only minutes before.

"Wow, sounds like all you folks are pretty resourceful," Wharton said. "Honestly, we're not sure what happened to our families. We hope for the best. Maybe they all ended up with good folks like you."

The three privates stared at the ground, the pain of not knowing churning inside them.

"And I don't mean to be all business, but facts are facts," Wharton said. "When those things start to swarm like that, it means they've taken notice of you. That's why they came down from the mountain."

"What do you recommend we do?" I asked.

"I noticed you have a little fishing boat out there. It's too small for all of us to leave in that, and our boat's disabled. You say you have a Lincoln Navigator?"

"Yes, we do," I said.

"Gas?"

"Three-quarters of a tank."

"That's enough to get us to resistance territory in the south," Wharton said. "Folks, I suggest we evacuate immediately. I know the highways around here. I'm sure you do, too. Between all of us, we should be able to fight off any bad folks along the way. The aliens keep away from the roads. What do you think?"

"Don't forget those people who left in my van," Kimberly said. "The aliens attacked it. Killed every one of them."

"Were they armed?" Wharton asked.

"I'm afraid not," I said. "But the sheer numbers I saw out there . . ."

Wharton turned to his men, "Maybe we ought to have a look."

I led them out front. Our shoulders sank when we saw the aliens massed along the front gate. They filed out along the side fences, working toward the back, surrounding us.

"In a few seconds, we'll be hemmed in," Fletcher said.

We ran toward the back. The aliens along the side fences kept up with us as we ran. We returned to the deck and found Kimberly and Jeff protecting Monica and the kids, aiming their weapons, wondering what to do next.

"Okay, looks like here is where we make our stand," Wharton said. "You guys know if we kill the mantis, all these things will lose whatever power is animating them."

"We know that," I said.

"The trick will be getting to the mantis," Kimberly said.

"Will the mantis come clear down here?" I asked Wharton.

"In my experience, no," he said. "We're going to have to fight our way to him,"

"I don't mean to be pessimistic after all we've been through," Jeff said. "But we're not gonna make it through all of them. We'll be goners before we take two steps up that path."

"If we're gonna do something, we'll have to do it now," I said. "They're not to the back gate yet. If we hurry through there, we can start up the path and take it up and around. I know the way. It leads to a pass approaching the mantis cave from the blindside."

"That's our best shot, then," Wharton said. "Those things can move fast, but we're faster. We'll draw them away from the house and up the path. Hopefully, we can turn that thing into Swiss cheese before they catch up."

"But we have to move now," Burton said.

"You folks want to wait here?" Wharton said. "Once we draw them off, you folks can drive out of here."

Kimberly and I exchanged looks with Jeff and Monica. I could tell Jeff felt an obligation to join the fight.

"Jeff, you stay with your family," I said. "Take everyone into the house. All the bedrooms have barricades. Pick one and lock yourselves in. Take some food with you. It's the best place to be until we come back for you."

"All right then," Jeff said. "If you don't get him, we're dead meat anyway."

Wharton and his men were already running toward the back fence.

I looked at Kimberly.

"They'll need us," I said.

"Then let's go," she said.

Events moved so fast that I didn't have a chance to tell Kimberly much. There would be no date night or slow dancing on the deck under the moonlight. The finality of events had caught up to us, and there was no time for anything but action. In a way, it was a relief. It would be over in a matter of minutes, life and death settled.

She smiled at me, another dazzler showing no fear. She was totally at peace with whatever was to come. She readied her weapon.

Jeff and Monica ran into the house as we followed Wharton and his men out the gate, around the corner of the fence, and up the path. I locked the gate. Kimberly waited with me. We caught up. Wharton and his men fired a few shots to get the aliens' attention. It worked.

They looked around, having finished with this group and looking for more prey. It was the most dangerous moment. Kimberly and I were slower than the soldiers but faster than the alien creatures. They skittered after us, making that weird clickety-clack sound, hundreds of them flowing after us like poisonous water seeking the easiest path.

THE MANTIS

We didn't have to run as fast as we thought. The creatures scrambled along, slow and steady, like a horde of giant cockroaches. Lord, they were disgusting. We didn't waste any ammunition on them right away.

"Remember, our goal is to take out that mantis," Wharton said. "Does it have a hiding place? Do you know?"

"It stays in a cave in the cliff wall," I said. "It can be drawn out if we make a ruckus."

"You've seen it and lived?" Wharton said, shaking his head. "You folks are a good-luck charm."

Wharton ran backward for a few steps, speaking to his men. "Then we're crashing the cave right away."

To us: "You two give us cover. Try to keep those things from swarming us. As soon as we kill the mantis, it's over."

We followed the path over the peak and down to the blind pass. We came around the trees at the bend and found the clearing and the empty corral. The sphere was still in the center, quiet and dark. Its smooth, pewter exterior reflected the hazy shape of our bodies coming toward it.

"Did it leave?" Mallory asked.

"Not likely," Wharton said. "Something's controlling those things. It's still here, somewhere."

"What about the things following us?" I asked.

The aliens were not far behind us, following our path. We could hear them coming.

"Let's move in on that cave, now!" Wharton said.

The four of them spread out, weapons raised, ready to attack. I felt a tentative burst of optimism, thinking that we might be close to a victory, close to the end. Wharton must've sensed my thoughts. He looked over his shoulder at us.

"Look alive for any surprises," he said.

As if he'd uttered a secret code, alien creatures dropped down from the trees, landing on all of us. We cursed and shouted as the aliens set upon us with claws and spiked tales. Everyone was disciplined enough not to fire wildly. We let go of our weapons, pulled out our blades, and worked desperately to free ourselves.

Two aliens landed right on my back, and immediately, I felt searing pain as their blades slashed at my arms, back, and chest. Kimberly looked up just as her attackers dropped. She backpedaled several steps away. They landed on the ground, momentarily stunned. She had the presence of mind to shoot them.

All I could do now was watch her fight them off because I had three of them swarming me. They worked hard to force me to the ground. My skin was slick with blood, but I didn't yet feel the gush of a severe wound. I knew if I fell, I was a dead man.

"Keep shooting 'em!" I yelled to Kimberly. "Stay on your feet no matter what!"

I fought off a surge of panic as I failed to shake the aliens. More were coming. I freed my Dad's Bowie knife and had better luck. I decapitated the one facing me. It dropped. I stomped at the one slashing at my calves until its skull caved in. I felt a needle poking my back, about to stab me. I ran backward into a tree, stunning it long enough to cut his head off, too. That was three down out of a couple hundred. I was already near exhaustion.

Wharton and his men trudged through the horde, taking their licks and shooting into the cave. They were effective with their shots, dropping aliens by the bushel.

Kimberly found an effective strategy. She backed away and carefully selected her shots. She was terrific. I didn't see her miss a single time. She shot them in the chest and the head. They dropped one at a time. They weren't focused on her, though. She was deemed less of a threat by backing away from the cave.

I adopted her strategy and moved away from the cave. This gave me a breather, just as I'd hoped. I joined Kimberly in picking off the aliens trying to swarm Wharton and his men. They were covered in blood and cuts but were tough, efficient fighters. They were hopelessly outnumbered, though. Kimberly and I could only get so close to them before we risked shooting one of them in the head.

Private Fletcher fell to the ground, still. I shouted at the surviving three, telling them that the aliens would relent in their attack if we pulled back. Wharton heard this. He turned to Mallory and Burton, shouting at them to retreat.

The three of them turned suddenly and ran away from the cave. The aliens were temporarily confused. They scattered around a bit with no rhyme or reason. Burton ran toward me. Mallory ran toward Kimberly.

Wharton stopped at the sphere and fired at it. I assume the bullets would ricochet off inside, but they penetrated. Out of the bullet holes came streams of blood, confirming Kimberly and I's theory that the spheres were the alien equivalent of oil tankers.

"Come on out! You filthy coward!" Wharton shouted.

He looked like a madman with his blood-covered face screaming in rage.

"Come and see me!" he said.

The aliens organized themselves into clusters, each focusing on one of us. I heard the aliens following us coming down the path toward the bend.

Wharton's men joined him in firing at the sphere. Geysers of blood sprayed in all directions like a giant, satanic showerhead. Blood covered everything and everyone, including the aliens. Once again, the aliens broke their organized ranks and wandered, confused. Perhaps the blood had some buzzing effect upon them, like a shot of tequila to us.

While the soldiers shot the sphere, Kimberly and I shot the aliens. We had a relatively easy time of it while they were disoriented.

The mantis appeared at the entrance to the cave. I almost laughed at how slow and lazily it moved, as if it were an old man awakened by a knock at his door. My mirth disappeared when I saw the weapon in its right hand.

Everyone saw it and knew that either we or the mantis would be dead in moments. I steeled myself for the end. Only seconds to live, now. We had done our best.

Seconds was all it took. The mantis brought the weapon up. The orb glowed red. The beam distorted the air as it started its sweep. The alien creatures sparked to attention once again. Since Wharton was the closest, he took the brunt of the attack. As he was swarmed, he put several rounds into the mantis's midsection. The creature was hurt but continued sweeping the weapon, catching Wharton in the beam. He grew drowsy, his eyes closing and opening until they closed for good. He staggered and fell to the ground.

The aliens swarmed Burton and me before we could take a shot at the mantis. I was numb with terror. Kimberly was away to my left. The beam's arc would catch her before me. She and Mallory were likewise swarmed with aliens, preventing them from raising their rifles.

The beam continued, enveloping Mallory. He dozed off as if he had been sung a sweet lullaby and fell to the ground. His attackers dropped away.

My eyes met Kimberly's as the wave swept across her. She shuddered, and I screamed in anguish. Heartbreak radiated through my extremities and numbed my fingertips. I swore and screamed with rage as I tore at my attackers.

Kimberly's eyes closed and opened. She tried to fight the effects of the oncoming sleep. She opened her eyes wide, trying to stay awake a little longer. She looked from me to the mantis. It continued its victory sweep toward me and Burton. We couldn't free our arms to fire.

Kimberly's aliens dropped away and ran toward us as if they could sense she was under the beam's effect. I screamed Kimberly's name, thinking it might keep her awake. She grew unsteady on her feet, staggering forward and backward, desperately trying to stay awake. She tried to raise her rifle at the mantis, but it was as if her arms were made of rubber.

The beam came closer to me. I was ready to welcome it now. I met Kimberly's eyes again. She gave me a weird smile, the kind of smile she always gave me when she had thought of something I hadn't. She gritted her teeth and managed to aim her rifle, only she aimed it at her foot and shot it.

Burton and I watched her in shock. We knew right away why she'd done it. The pain and adrenaline burst of the sudden blast through her foot gave her added consciousness. I felt the vibration of the beam coming close. My guts fluttered. My hair stood on end.

Kimberly used the energy boost to raise her rifle and shoot the mantis's weapon to pieces along with its arm. The mantis looked at its mangled stump. Kimberly collapsed to the ground, still keeping her eyes open.

Inspired, Burton and I broke free. We fired at the mantis and turned it into a dead mess so hideous I would never eat pasta again. When it was dead, aliens surrounding us suddenly dropped to the ground. They rolled and writhed until they lay still on their backs like dead spiders, twitching and making weird noises.

Burton and I rushed to Kimberly. I gathered her in my arms. She fought to stay awake, opening her eyes wide before they would slowly shut, and she would open them again. I glanced up at Burton, hoping he would have an answer. His face was sad. He had no solutions. I looked back down to Kimberly. She looked at me, recognizing me.

"We won, babe!" I said, wanting her to know that. "We killed it!"

She smiled widely. Not even the blood and dirt staining her face could stop her from looking as beautiful as I've ever seen her.

"I love you," she said, groggy.

I picked her up and stood to my feet. We ran back toward the house. Burton followed. Over the hill and down was the fastest way to go. It played hell on my thighs. I shook Kimberly when her eyes shut, and they fluttered open again. She sang to keep her mind active. She mostly mumbled off-key. It was the best vocal performance I ever heard.

We reached the side fence and turned west, running toward the ocean. We passed dozens of inert aliens. Jeff and Monica saw us. They cheered and shook their fists. They had seen the aliens drop to the ground and knew what it meant. They sobered up when they saw me carrying Kimberly.

We burst out onto the beach. I ran to where the tide splashed in and dropped to my knees, still holding her. The Kiplers gathered near us. Monica was crying. Burton and Jeff were grim. They took a knee next to us. Kimberly mumbled something I couldn't understand. I leaned in and put my ear to her lips.

"Squeeze my foot," she mumbled.

Her injured foot. I squeezed it, and her eyes popped open from the pain. She looked around, disoriented for a moment. I touched her cheek and guided her gaze to mine. She smiled again.

"This is . . . how I would have chosen it to end . . . here . . . in your arms."

"There's got to be something we can do," I said.

No one answered.

'Thank you for showing me . . . that it's okay to take another chance . . . on love."

Her words were slurred and sleepy.

"You'll always remember that . . . won't you?"

"I'll remember," I said, barely able to talk. "I'll remember everything."

She closed her eyes for the final time.

"Until . . . we sleep . . ."

With a sweet smile on her face, she was gone.

I sat for a moment, feeling the waves swirl around me. Burton squeezed my shoulder. The others gathered close. I stroked her cheek, and we sat silently together.

I looked out to the horizon, considering the ancient indifference of the ocean.

UNTIL WE SLEEP

Monica and her daughters did a lovely job getting Kimberly ready. They dressed her in the teal summer dress, fixed her hair, gave her a manicure and a pedicure, and bound up the wound on her foot. The flower crown I made for her on our wedding day rested on the nightstand. It was withered and drying out, but I gave it to them, and they put it on her.

There were two coffins left from Dad's work way back when. They had been meant for us. I had moved them to the garage and thought about bringing one out for Kimberly. I abandoned the idea. It didn't seem like what she would want.

When she was fixed and fancy, I carried her to the tower and placed her on the bed. It was evening by then. I didn't want to take her to sea in the dark, so it would have to be done soon. I sat by the bed for a long while, waiting for tears to come and start the emotional purge. It never happened, though. I couldn't say I was shocked. The odds were best that one of us would say goodbye like this. I just held her hand. It had grown cold, and it seemed unnatural and unfair. So, I folded her hands over her chest and let her lie there.

Burton entered the room after a while.

"Sorry to interrupt," he said.

"It's okay," I said. "I think I'm ready. Everyone else okay?"

"Fine," he said. "I think we should evacuate the property as soon as we've said goodbye to Kimberly."

"Really? I thought the crisis had passed."

"The death of the mantis won't pass unnoticed," he said. "Not only will the alien race want to know what happened, but our corrupt government will come looking for answers."

"No rest for the weary," I said. "You told Jeff and Monica?"

"Yes. They'll come with us," he said. "If we can reach the resistance border, we might just get some rest. Maybe even a steak and a beer."

I stood up. "You've sold me. Okay, I'll bring her down now."

I came out to see Monica grilling fish. Jeff and Burton had managed a decent catch. She found some canned vegetables and pudding.

"Go ahead and do what you must, Colby," she said. "Then we'll have a nice dinner before we go."

"We won, my friends," I said. "Thank you. She would want us to celebrate. If the roles had been reversed, she would get drunk and party. She told me so."

They laughed. As I passed by with her, everyone touched her hair, hand, or shoulder, thanking her for what she'd done and wishing her peace on her journey to Heaven.

I carried Kimberly onto the beach. The others followed me quietly. I had no plan for a service. After a few seconds of quiet, Burton offered to say a few words. He delivered a lovely prayer, expressing thanks for the victory we had won, thankfulness for Kimberly's life, and for the future she's given us.

I rested her head in my lap as I motored out until the others were tiny dots on the sand. I killed the motor, and we bounced on the waves a while. I ran my fingers over her arms and face and through the thickness of her hair. I committed every detail to memory.

"You're not going to wake up, are you?" I asked.

When I had waited long enough, I took her in my arms, held her over the boat's edge, and released her into the sea. She floated on the surface for a moment with her arms spread out and her peaceful, beautiful face looking up at the sky through closed eyes. Slowly, she went under, feet first. Seconds later, her head and hands slipped below. I leaned over the edge. In the depths, I saw the whiteness of her skin and the chestnut of her hair fanning out as if she traveled through space on her way to heaven.

"Until we sleep, my love."

I kept watch until she faded away.

Burton did most of the talking as we drove. It was nice to focus my mind on practicalities. He was the one with all the knowledge. We questioned him relentlessly.

The resistance was real and formidable. They were reclaiming territory throughout the United States. He couldn't speak for the rest of the world but wouldn't be surprised if people rebelled in other countries. Not only were they reclaiming territory, they were shooting spheres down from the sky. They could have been shot down by the Air Force all along, but orders had been given for our planes to stand down. The invasion had come with the cooperation of our leaders.

"This kind of betrayal," I said. "Hell is too good."

"Plans are in place to settle accounts," Burton said. "Local leaders have already been to the noose."

Resistance territory was about fifty miles south of where we were. It was not a long drive in normal days but a perilous journey in chaotic times. Burton wasn't worried. He felt that the four adults, armed, in a gassed-up Navigator, should be okay.

He asked me how well I knew the out-of-the-way roads and highways. My Dad had been fond of taking back roads. I had learned to drive out here. Taking the back way to resistance territory would not be a problem. The journey down to resistance territory was uneventful. Peaceful, actually. After the tension of the first thirty minutes waiting to be attacked, I allowed myself to relax and feel the aching numbness in my heart.

Joni and the Kipler girls entertained us by acting out their favorite movies. And when I say they acted them out, I mean they acted out the entire thing — every line of dialogue, every action, described every visual of every scene. It was delightful. I laughed so hard. It was my first experience wishing Kimberly was with me to see it.

After an hour and a half on the road, we encountered a checkpoint across the highway. I glanced at Burton, wondering what to do. He looked concerned for a moment, then relaxed.

"That's our boys!" He said. "We made it!"

We were admitted into the territory. Two soldiers in a Jeep escorted us into a medium-sized town. There was a community center where we were taken for processing. I was impressed by the system they had set up. There was little doubt the forces behind the resistance had been high-ranking government officials and soldiers. Thank God some good guys in power did the right thing.

We were each sent to a table where officials with laptop computers asked us a series of questions. They had access to whatever relevant databases they needed because they could confirm my identity. They inquired about my family, and I told them that Leo, Robyn, Madison, and Sophia Swanson were all dead. I informed them the Maris family had been with us when we were attacked, and that they were also dead.

I kept Kimberly and I's marriage to myself. I had no documentation of it and worried it would look suspicious. Another reason was that speaking of her in the past tense twisted my guts.

After my questioning, I was sent on to a man and a woman in a partitioned room. Their job was to take care of the legalities of getting people's property and money sorted in the aftermath of the chaos.

"It's a good thing you still have your wallet," the man, Gil, said. "Most people have lost everything. Will take a long time to verify who they are and what assets they have."

"Computers are still up?" I asked.

"Our leaders were partners in the alien invasion," the woman, Andrea, said. "They kept infrastructure in place, for the most part. It was to their benefit to keep electronics and banking up and running."

"I heard they put people with A-positive blood in critical jobs," I said. "That true?"

"Appears to be," Gil said.

"Mr. Swanson, you have considerable assets," Andrea said. "Your parents' estate is all yours. The property—a house and office building in Seattle and a house on the ocean—are still in occupied territory, but all bank accounts, stocks, and insurance benefits are at your disposal now."

"How long before everything is liberated?" I asked.

"Hard to say," Gil said. "But your property is on a list. When the areas are cleared and stabilized, you can do with them what you want."

"In the meantime, you have more options than most," Andrea said. "There's plenty of room in the gymnasiums and churches, but we encourage those with access to their money to rent a house or an apartment."

"We'll send you to a realtor," Gil said.

They smiled at me as if the meeting had concluded happily.

"Um, what am I expected to do now?" I asked.

"Well, we're satisfied with our recruitment goals for the army," Gil said.

I was glad to hear that. I felt my fighting days were over, and I was ready to move on.

'What we really need is for people to start moving on," Andrea said. "You know, get married, have kids, build things. Start living again!"

It was hard to believe how well things had gone. I turned to tell Kimberly. I had become so used to her being next to me. But I was alone and dreaded the day I would get used to it.

I found the Kiplers at a shelter in a church. Monica hugged me tight.

"Can you believe we made it?" she asked. "How are you doing?"

We caught each other up on events since we arrived.

"We had a long talk with Joni," she said. "We're going to adopt her."

"That's great!" I said. "It can be arranged?"

"There are lots of orphans," Jeff said. "We'll have to be vetted, and they'll search for relatives, but they'll okay it."

'Are you guys staying here?" I asked.

"Until they can verify our identities," Jeff said.

"I'm on my way to meet a realtor," I said. "What say we get a house together? I'd hate to live alone."

We found a handsome corner house, an immense brick beauty with plenty of room for me, the Kiplers, and their three girls. Jeff and Monica found jobs in town. I took my first tentative steps toward building tables and chairs.

Private Burton stopped by to see us and say goodbye. He was back with his unit and returning to the fight. The resistance was gaining momentum, and an assault on Seattle was soon to begin. I told him he could have my house once the city was retaken. He laughed. I wasn't kidding. He said that was good motivation to win. He high-fived the girls and walked away.

Soon enough, the Kipler's home in Oregon was liberated, and they were off to start their lives anew. I sold the big house and moved into a smaller one.

Life went on for all of us. Time would tolerate nothing else.

BEGINNINGS

One year later, I received a call from Burton telling me they had reclaimed the beach house. He was Lieutenant Burton by then. He had his men fix up the property, even going so far as to give it another coat of paint. He had the fences repaired, and the deck sanded and re-stained. They combed through Blackjack Hill, removed all alien carcasses, and burned them. Special equipment was brought in to remove the sphere. He remembered what I had told him about Solomon's slave camp in the north. Even though Solomon was dead, I suspected his operation still functioned. In a wink-wink tone, Burton told me there were no more pirates.

All was back to normal, he said. I could return anytime I wanted.

The idea of going back to the beach house without Kimberly felt like somebody sinking a drill into my heart. I arranged to rent it out. I had a couple of longtime tenants who kept the place full of life and treated it well.

I was thirty—eleven years after the alien attack—when the fight was won for good. New leadership took over the federal government. All states had elected a proper governor and legislature. Curious how fast and slow those eleven years went by.

I stayed in Calico, the city we came to when we fled the house. Over time, I slowly but surely built a prosperous woodworking business. I made tables and chairs, mostly. I shipped them all over the United States. Soon, I had a towering house and a spacious woodworking shop on an acreage, just like the man who had inspired me so long ago.

After the world had stabilized, more or less, I felt that the pause button on my life had finally been released. I began to look around me and pay attention to what God put in my path. That's when I met Corinna. She was my age. Like everyone, her body was crisscrossed with scars inside and out. It was a cautious beginning—long walks and safe conversations, leading to more and more time together, giving way to gathering the courage to talk about the future, a shared future. When my feelings stirred for Corinna, it naturally dropped me back into a lap of grief that I felt for Kimberly.

I talked about this with Corinna. She had the same feelings stirred up about the boyfriend she had and lost. It was expected, she said.

Kimberly had become a bittersweet, melancholy memory for me by then. I thought about her occasionally, but bringing up thoughts of her on my own was too painful. I let her drift in and out of my thoughts as she pleased. But when Corinna came along, thoughts of Kimberly receded. I have a feeling Kimberly caused this retreat herself, from her vantage point above, as a way to tell me it was time to let the past be the past. I remembered Kimberly's last words to me—that taking one more chance on love was good and right.

I was forty-five when I came to the beach house for the first time since I'd left. Burton and the Kiplers had faded away from me. We represented painful memories to each other. We had survived together, but trauma was our uniting force. It couldn't be sustained.

Corinna knew about the house. I told her I wanted to move us and the business up to the beach house when the time was right. That had been my original plan all along before things went wrong. I made good on my promise to Burton to give him my house. I sold the office building. That, along with the money I had inherited from Mom and Dad, left us in a comfortable position for the rest of our lives.

We drove north along familiar highways. Corinna and I only talked off and on. There was no tension between us. She was happy and content, riding with the windows down, feeling the wind blow through her blonde hair, and listening to the sounds of our two daughters in the backseat.

They were twins, ten years old at the time. We named them Robyn, after my mother, and Melanie, after Corinna's. Neither of our mothers had survived the invasion, nor had our fathers. Like me, she was the only survivor of her family.

I drove down the winding path to the house. It was Fall, and the leaves were gold and brown, the air cool. I checked for some sign of that old burnt-out truck that Dad and I had set on fire. It was gone. I'm sure Burton had his men pull it out of there.

The gate's padlock had been left open, just as the realtor promised. I pushed the gate open, drove through, and closed it again. I secured it with my padlock. We parked in front of the house. The girls bounded out of the vehicle just as my sisters did when my family had arrived for the last time.

Corinna was overwhelmed by the beauty of the old place. She had accepted, on my word, that this would be an appropriate place for our family to move. I don't think it had been painted since Burton's men had done it. It was ready for another coat. That would give me a fall project. Corinna looked away from the house to me and smiled. I was home, and so was she.

The girls had never seen the ocean before. I led them around the side of the house. Emotions surged hard when we came around the house and onto the old deck. I paused to look around. Memories of my incredible summer here converged at once—the terror, the pain, the loss, and most importantly, the love Kimberly and I shared in the shadow of death.

Corinna knew of my experiences here. I had told her of Kimberly. It didn't seem right to keep it from her. I didn't give a lot of details. We had agreed to keep the specifics of our time in the dark days to ourselves. The past is the past. We had pledged our lives together in the name of constantly moving forward.

We weren't the only ones who had to keep a balm on open wounds. Indeed, the whole world was still recovering. The shared psychic gash was still raw. Giant cemeteries were everywhere. Tribunals for traitors still took place. We looked at each other sometimes, wondering what our secrets were in this mess.

We had to jog to keep up with the girls as they led us to the beach.

The girls ran delighted into the water, splashing around and squealing with delight. Corinna tried to keep them from running out too far. The life and energy they brought was so powerful I wished I could reach back in time to tell my younger self that all would be well. I drifted away from them, wanting a few seconds to myself.

Ghosts surrounded me. Sounds and images. Dad's gregarious laugh and endless stream of wisdom. Mom's beauty and the comfort of her warm embrace. Sophia and her intense curiosity. Madison and the imagination that powered her art and writing. All gone, yet still here.

The sand under my feet felt no different than when I returned from releasing Kimberly into the sea. It had been so long, she seemed as morning mist to me. I looked around me, regarding the house, deck, and trail going up Blackjack Hill. Nothing had changed. It was real, and it was there, just as I was.

I had no physical memento of Kimberly. No clothing, no lock of hair. When I let her go, I had let her go. We had no marriage certificate, as we had made our promise before God and each other and called it good. There was no picture of us together as husband and wife.

Kimberly never even officially had my last name. The official records of bureaucracy and government officially remember her as the wife of Philip Maris and mother to Sebastian and Lydia. I have no quarrel with that. The love we shared is remembered only as long as I have a sound mind. When I am gone, all we had together will enter eternity.

The waves crashed hard as the tide roared in. There was an urgency to the rolling water, as if it called to me, demanding I remember. I questioned my sanity for a moment when I heard her singing. Naturally, I thought it was just a memory ringing in my head. But when I concentrated, I knew the sound came from the water, floating to me in the air just like the waves' hiss and the birds' calling. I whispered a quick prayer to God, thanking him for allowing her to sing to me one more time.

I allow the pain of losing her to grip me one more time. I am grateful for the sting of it, and I smile.

"Kimberly."

I could barely choke out her name, but I had to say it and hear it one more time.

The sounds of family overtook me then. I looked over at them, waved, and smiled. I look again to Blackjack Hill, home of Blackjack Rane Cooper, who supposedly buried a treasure there I was determined to find but never did.

I walked back toward my family, and my children ran to me.

About the Author

James B. Christensen is the author of *The Vessel,* an occult horror thriller, *Honeymoon Phase,* a supernatural romantic comedy, and the *October Nights* anthology series. He lives in Omaha with his family.

Find these books and visit James at jamesbchristensen.com.